TOO DANGEROUS TO LIVE

"It comes down to this," Stain went on. "We cannot let Tom Horn go." He looked dramatically around the room, his chin uplifted, and allowed the statement to sink in.

"So what'll we do, John?" said James. "Let him hang and let the accusations make their way to the law in Denver?"

"No, of course not, Dave," answered Stain. "But I think I do have a plan. If we allow Horn his freedom, he'll brag and bluster about his days as a stock detective and how he saw the light after his deceitful employers framed him for the killing of a child."

"It seems like we're back between a rock and a hard spot," said Cooper. "You said you and Ford had come up with some plan. Spit it out."

Stain smiled at Cooper's bluntness and continued. "We just need to play along and let Horn out of the trap. Everything can go according to plan. We'll stage the hanging, slip Horn out a few miles to Coble's spread, show him the money and give him a horse. When he thinks he's free . . ."—Stain paused for effect—"we'll have to kill him."

WYOMING WIND

A Novel of Tom Horn

JON CHANDLER

LEISURE BOOKS NEW YORK CITY

To my parents, Helen and Verdon.

A LEISURE BOOK®

May 2003

Published by

Dorchester Publishing Co., Inc.
276 Fifth Avenue
New York, NY 10001

ISBN: 0-8439-5165-6

Printed in the United States of America.

Visit us on the web at www.dorchesterpub.com.

WYOMING WIND

A Novel of Tom Horn

As far as actual killing is concerned, I never killed a man in my life, or a boy either.

Tom Horn

The first time I met the girl was just before the killing of the kid. Everything, you know, dates from the killing of the kid.

Tom Horn

Prologue

Cheyenne, Wyoming, 2002

The small bar in downtown Cheyenne was tucked between two Victorian buildings, each extending two stories above it, giving the short city block the look of a gap-toothed smile. The exterior had been renovated, the old rust-red bricks sandblasted and cleaned. The expensive sign, lettered to resemble an 1890s counterpart, projected the place as being friendly and safe.

The interior decor was a schizophrenic combination of Old West and East Coast urban. Posters featuring scantily clad young women, displaying frosty bottles of beer, bedecked the walls, incongruous and silly above the century-old carved wooden booths. A neon HEINEKEN sign was placed next to a plaque that proclaimed the two holes in the wall, directly above, came about as the result of an 1897 gun battle between two cowboys in from the range. According to the plaque, both died and were buried on the prairie.

The massive hardwood bar itself was the work of a master craftsman. Commissioned in 1895 for a billiard hall and gambling establishment called The Dove, the finished product was sent west by rail from Chicago nearly two years later. When the city of Cheyenne closed The Dove for being a nuisance, the wooden bar itself was moved to its present location.

Ornately carved and mirrored, the oaken back-bar and its matching serving counter, complete with brass rails and spittoons, had absorbed nearly a century of cigar and cigarette smoke. With its various nicks and scratches, the old darkening varnish became as well known to patrons as the wrinkles on their faces.

In 1980, the bar's owner, Ernie Stanton, decided to upgrade the establishment—his contribution to a new sense of civic pride and urban renewal. He also figured the move to fern bars that was sweeping the country would benefit him. In that era it was reasoned that such bars attracted women, who ostensibly felt they were safely ensconced in a habitat that radiated respectability, perhaps akin to drinking fuzzy navels in a doctor's office. Of course, women attracted men. A lot of liquor was sold.

As the fern bar craze abated, the owner retained the concept of serving good food and slightly expensive drinks, while wisely throwing the greenery out the back door into the alley. The only long-term effect of the fern bar fad was the beautifully refinished bar dominating the room. Its original rich maple color was restored during that period in order to brighten up the place. Its nicks and scratches were expertly eradicated. Ernie Stanton fell in love with it. It was work to be proud of, and it drew those who sought a feel for the 19th Century through the door and back in time.

The local and the visitor were sitting on stout brass-ringed stools, facing the bar, with their elbows on the counter. They stared into the back-bar's massive mirror as they sipped their Coors longnecks. Both were dressed in blue jeans, but the similarity ended there. The local's bushy salt-and-pepper moustache, tanned face, and comfortable elk-skin boots branded him as pure Wyoming. He had worn a short-brimmed cowboy hat into the bar, hanging it on the hatrack inside the door. His voice sounded like an ad for Marlboro smokes, and he had the habit of pulling on one side of his moustache.

The clean-shaven visitor sported a short, silk jacket and wore expensive cologne. His hiking boots were obviously new. His accent pegged him as East Coast, once removed, Southern California now. He was a good businessman and was glad the local had turned out to have a fine business mind.

They started out talking about the potential for raising hormone free cattle and bison over lunch at a table in the corner. A couple of hours later, a preliminary deal was struck, and they walked to the bar to wind down, to see if perhaps they could be friends as well as business associates.

The men talked about Wyoming's economy and how the state would face new challenges common to the West, challenges that were fast reshaping both social and economic conventions. As is true in most such conversations, talk of the future inevitably led to talk of the past.

"This place is amazing," said the visitor. "I feel like I'm in a theme park."

The local laughed out loud.

Pointing to the bullet holes in the wall, the visitor stated: "So, two cowboys really met their maker right here. Wow. Who was it got shot?"

"Maybe a cockroach or two," chuckled the local. "That's about all.

"Rumor says Ernie's dad pulled out a Forty-Four after the Second World War and blasted the wall so tourists'd think they were in the authentic West."

The visitor shook his head and guffawed.

"So it's just a scam, huh?" he chuckled. "Kind of a 'Buffalo Bill slept here' deal?"

"Yeah, I s'pose," said the local. "But it's more likely Bill slept in the cathouse next door."

The two laughed as the local expanded on the image of old Cody enjoying the charms available at Madam Wren's. A discreet businesswoman, the crafty Delilah Wren had catered to cowboys and English nobles, famous gunmen, and railroad barons alike, before moving her business to Denver in 1910.

The local took a sip of Rocky Mountain spring water, got a serious look on his face, and continued. "You know, this place really does have a pretty interestin' history. A lot of the cattle barons who built Wyoming used to drink here. So did ol' Tom Horn."

"Man," the visitor uttered. "*The* Tom Horn? The famous whatchamacallit . . ."—he stumbled for the word—"dry-gulcher? That's it. They made a movie about him, didn't they?"

"Oh, yeah," the local responded with a wry grin.

The visitor thought for a moment, swallowed a sip of beer, and said: "I read they retried him a couple of years or so back, didn't I? There was something in one of those United flight mags. Found him not guilty of killing some kid? That right?"

"That's what they said," the local laughed. "Doesn't do ol' Tom too much good ninety-five years after the fact. Aw, I guess it gives some sticklers for accuracy in jurisprudence comfort, but it's all academic. Horn sure as heck got what he deserved."

"Whaddya mean, like his confession was hearsay, but he really did it?" asked the visitor.

"Well, maybe. There's a lot of controversy about the kid, Willie Nickell was his name . . . who killed him, that sorta thing. Willie's dad was gut-shot mean, and most folks then and now figure someone was after him and shot Willie by mistake. Most people think it was probably Horn, but a lot of others say it was the cattlemen he worked for, tryin' to frame him. He was becomin' a big P.R. problem for 'em."

"The Johnson County War cattlemen?"

"Um, not exactly, 'cause the Johnson County War was a few years earlier. But pretty much the same type of fellas. Those guys owned huge ranches all over Wyoming and Montana and even down into Colorado. In fact my great-grandfather, Pete Cooper, was one of the biggest around here." The local raised his eyebrows and uttered a wry chuckle. "Yep, he knew ol' Tom real well."

"So your great-grandpa was one of the bad guys, huh?" mused the visitor.

"Well, it all depends on how you look at it. Rustlers were stealin' the cattlemen blind, and sheep were eatin' their grass. They were arrogant s.o.b.s, all right, so they did what arrogant people do. They tried to force rustlers and sheepmen out. If they didn't go, Tom Horn and a few others like him killed 'em. Simple as that."

The visitor fiddled with some loose change on the counter, trying to recall some bit of information he had heard. He spun a quarter on the bar at a dizzying pace and gently lowered his index finger, capturing it upright. He said: "You know, I *do* remember the legend of Horn. He took secrets to the grave, stood by his friends, all of that."

"That's what they say."

"So, where'd they hang him? Is it near here?"

The local surveyed the several dozen or so liquor bottles placed on the back-bar for a moment, then turned a determined look on the visitor.

"I think you and I are gonna have a pretty good relationship on down the road, so I'm inclined to tell you a few things I generally keep quiet. You wanna know what *really* happened here? About hangin's and such? I'll tell you what my grandfather told me. He was told by his father, who was there. Look at the pictures, read the reports, he was there."

The local took a long pull from the longneck bottle, smiled to himself, and began. "Long about Nineteen-Oh-One, Horn was gettin' himself a pretty bad name. He'd been an Army scout and interpreter in the Apache wars down in Arizona. Worked for George Crook and Nelson Miles, it's said. Fact is he always held that he was the one who accepted Geronimo's final surrender. Maybe so.

"Everything changed after that. Indians were on reservations, and even the roughest towns were gettin' civilized. Horn apparently felt the Wild West was gone, which it prob'ly was. So, he managed to become an assassin, shootin' rustlers and sheepmen for the big cattle interests.

"He was wild and many thought out of control. Then the kid turned up dead. . . ."

Chapter One

Cheyenne, Wyoming, 1903

The wind is all.

The wind is ever present.

The wind fashions life on the desolate prairie. In this domain every living thing knows the wind's power, and each is subjugated accordingly.

The few seedlings that survive the constant gusts and grow into willow and scrub oak lean to the east, trying to uproot themselves—trying to avoid the wind as a young woman avoids the advances of an unwelcome suitor.

The prairie grasses wave like sheets of pure green silk over the soft, rolling hills. The wind plays the new grass in springtime like a billion reeds. An indescribable symphony arises from the prairie. Lonesome, forsaken, yet compelling and ultimately enrapturing.

The pronghorn face the west wind, daring it to blow harder. Their impassive faces carry the pattern of the prairie, the white, black, and brown of the high lonesome. Proud to the point of arrogance, they use the wind to smell out danger, to foretell difficult weather. They stand like monuments, challenging the wind's power. Yet, even they are betrayed when the predator's scent is hidden, allowing death to approach from downwind.

The raptors know the wind, and have learned to use it.

The golden eagle and red-tailed hawk ride its currents on their endless search for prey. They sail into the wind, returning its pressure, and from the earth below seem immobile high in the brilliant blue sky. They use the wind as a tool, a silent adjunct to their swift and constant killing.

Slowly, inexorably, the wind chips away at the wood and brick buildings that so quickly and unexpectedly grew from the ancient prairie. Like its cousin the water, the wind washes over the creations of man, stripping them of form and substance.

Yet, Cheyenne is defiant. Born of the Union Pacific's intercontinental ribbon of steel and bred by the sheer power of the West's cattlemen, it is a venerable adversary.

Cheyenne's people know the Wyoming wind. Its force is like some horizontal gravity, and they learn to walk subject to it. Before leaving their dwellings, they grab their hats and pull their scarves across their faces. When they return, they cough the wind-born dust from their lungs. They sway imperceptibly when inside shelter, unconsciously dancing to the wind's rhythms.

They trust the wind, knowing it is always there.

They suspect the wind, feeling its sheer potency.

The wind can soothe, or bring madness.

Like a rider on the horizon, the wind is a messenger.

And now, from the northwest, the wind brings more than clouds and dust.

It brings betrayal and murder.

He wasn't sure where he was. The town looked familiar, and he thought it might be in Wyoming, but everything seemed wrong. He couldn't identify any buildings, or any people for that matter. No, this didn't look like Cheyenne, or even Casper. And it sure wasn't down Colorado way, Greeley or Denver.

The boardwalks looked brand new, the bare wood bright and splintery, still oozing sap. There were no hitching posts, which he thought to be strange. The absence of road apples was stranger still. He supposed all the town's horses were stabled.

The clean red brick buildings seemed high and foreboding, with barred windows hiding their interior secrets.

Two women walking across the packed dirt street in front of him looked wonderfully fresh, their dresses pressed, their hair shining. Their open, frank gazes unnerved him, and he found he couldn't return their stares.

He realized he was walking down the center of the town's main street, flanked on both sides by tall men with long moustaches, wearing black broadcloth suits and broad-brimmed hats. Their unbuttoned coats flapped open as they walked, revealing well-worn hard maple pistol grips emerging from black leather holsters. They looked familiar, he thought, like illustrations he'd seen of the Earps in their Arizona days.

His arms were bound behind him with what seemed like smooth rope rather than steel handcuffs. The men guided him with firm hands grasping his upper arms. He had no idea where they were going, or why, but he felt the purpose to be dreadful.

He was a prisoner.

The sun cast a metallic light on the main street, and the long westward-pointing shadows indicated it was early morning. As they walked, he looked at the man to his right with a questioning glance but received only a steely stare in return.

They walked in silence for what seemed like hours, the only sound that of his captors' spurs jingling with each step. Once he thought he saw Coble behind a half-shuttered window. But he wasn't sure.

He heard a repeated noise, like a door slamming open into a wall. He looked behind him to see where it was coming from, and saw the crowd following; fifty, maybe sixty quiet people, led by a silver-haired man who looked like a judge or politician of some sort. The exquisitely dressed man rode in an eerily silent automobile, looking like captured prey in the jaws of a giant metallic insect.

While he was looking over his shoulder, the black automobile stopped, and the people crowded in around it, each staring ahead, above, and beyond him. Some began to point.

He snapped his head around and realized he was now inside a darkened building, perhaps a barn, lit only by shafts of sunlight slicing through heavily barred windows. His heart leaped into his throat as he found a gallows directly before him, rising up like a newly framed house. Now he recognized the noise. The gallows' trap door was being tested on the platform by a small figure dressed in a gray shirt, oversize, sloppy trousers, and black suspenders.

The kid.

He would spring the trap, letting it fall, then pull it back up with a rope looped through a crudely drilled hole in the platform's planks. Each time, he pulled a small oilcan from his pocket and lubricated the trap door's hinges. His sandy hair fell across his forehead, and he frequently brushed it from his eyes. He had the grave expression of someone determined to do a significant, meaningful job.

Apparently satisfied with the hinges, the boy pulled the door up, latched it, and walked to the edge of the scaffold, where a few steps were connected. He looked down and motioned to the silent men, who began escorting their charge toward the structure.

The boy stood at the top of the stairs, his arm extended, holding a black hood. He was smiling, his eyes glinting, reflecting the sun now pouring through a large window. Looking into the boy's eyes, the prisoner thought perhaps they were on fire.

The silent men grabbed his arms tighter, forcing him up the steps. He tried to resist, but found himself totally incapacitated, unable to exert any force whatsoever.

He looked up and saw the boy was holding the long rope leading to the noose. Grinning and chuckling now, the boy lovingly held the noose, stroking it, as the grim party ascended the steps.

Funny, he thought. I didn't know that kid could laugh.

Horn moaned softly. A quick, involuntary intake of breath woke him, causing him to clear his throat. Startled, his eyes opened wide, and he fought to remember where he was. He shook his head slightly and sat up carefully on the edge of the cot.

The dream that had gripped him seemed to hang in the air, and he again shook his head, harder this time, to eradicate the images. He was drenched in sweat, and his lean frame began to shiver in the early morning chill.

"Hmm, Willie-boy," he whispered aloud. "One-uh these nights you're mebbe gonna get me."

He pushed himself from the cot and stood, walking the two paces to the metal wash basin that lay on the short metal stand bolted to the cell wall. He leaned over and splashed water on his face, then quickly ran his fingers through his thinning hair, straight back.

Fully awake now and losing the dream, he stood upright and leaned back against the brick wall. For the thousandth time, he took in his surroundings: an eight-by-eight brick room with a thick wooden door serving as the only access. A small paneless window in the door held two thick metal bars, identical to those set into the somewhat larger window that allowed minimal light into the cell. A small tin latrine was stuffed into a corner, as far from the cot as possible.

The wash basin and metal water bucket and dipper were the only furnishings.

The outer window was too small for a man to crawl through, providing he could break the thick glass and then remove the five-foot long bars walled between two layers of brick. Of course, once that was accomplished, he'd have to jump down two stories onto the rickety wooden roof of an adjacent stable. Not that he hadn't thought about it. But then thinking wasn't his strong suit these days. If he'd been thinking instead of drinking, he'd be a thousand miles away, back in Arizona or even in some Mexican *cantina* spending the Wyoming Stock Growers Association's money.

He turned and walked back to the cot, sitting down on the edge with his head in his hands. He refused to stand and pace the cell. He felt it to be undignified.

He'd visited a zoological garden once in St. Louis. The zoo had a great tiger from India that lived in a huge cage, set apart from spectators by a moat filled with brackish green water. Horn had sat on an exposed rock near the cage and watched the tiger for two hours as it paced back and forth in front of an eighteen foot high cast-iron fence. It never once varied its regimen, never rested, never stopped. It just paced. Now, sitting on a prison cot in Cheyenne, he wished he would have shot it.

Horn sat quietly for the next hour, watching the cell grow brighter as the sun flooded the east-facing window. He heard movement in the adjacent room and stood to prepare himself for his morning meal.

"Awright, Tom," a voice boomed through the opening in the door. "You know what to do."

Horn stared for a moment at the door, then turned and leaned against the brick wall, spreading his arms and legs.

Clay Stephens peered through the opening, then unlocked the door and entered the cell with a plate of cold biscuits and gravy. He set the plate down on the cot and then backed out of the cell, firmly closing and locking the door.

Cheyenne's sheriff for the past three years, Stephens had a reputation as a careful and politically connected man. He was not about to be overpowered by a two-bit dry-gulcher in his own jail.

When Stephens exited, Horn turned and spoke loudly through the door's opening. "What're you doin' here? Where's that roustabout you call a deputy?"

"Thought I'd grace you with my presence," answered the sheriff.

"Haven't seen you in a coupla days!" Horn yelled.

Stephens laughed outside the door. "Figured I'd better check you out and make sure you're fit enough to be hanged next week."

"That's some sense of humor you got, Sheriff," said Horn. "Why don't you just slip me a Colt and I'll finish the job right here so's you can have your own private laugh?"

"Nope," chuckled Stephens. "I had to have Walt Conway's brains removed from the wall after that gal he was seein' smuggled him that Smith and Wesson. Warn't no fun at all."

Stephens paused for a while, but Horn could sense him still in position on the other side of the door. Obviously close to the door, the lawman spoke directly through the crack. "Got a message for you. John Stain's gonna drop by this morning."

" 'Bout time," answered Horn. "The little worm can't hide behind the governor's skirts much longer." He paused and ran his fingertips along the brick wall. "I was beginning to wonder if you'd even delivered my message."

"Oh, yeah, I did," said Stephens. "You sure shook the cattlemen up, all right. There was lights burning late and voices bein' raised all over the county. If I didn't know any better, I'd say there may be some plan afoot to prevent you from receiving your just due at the end of a rope."

"What would you know about justice?" Horn responded with a smirk. "You've killed more men in back alleys than I ever shot with a Winchester."

"Yeah, mebbe you're right, Tom," answered Stephens softly. "But I never bushwhacked no kid."

Horn immediately picked up the plate from the cot and hurled it at the door.

"There you go," he heard Stephens's amused voice retreating, laughing as he walked away. "More vittles for the rats 'n' roaches."

Horn slowly sat on the cot, getting control of himself. He stared at the slop dripping down the door and breathed deeply. He tried unsuccessfully to ban the taunt from his mind. But it came back, ever louder.

I never bushwhacked no kid.

Chapter Two

Horn sat immobile, watching infinitesimal motes of dust make their way through a spear of light slanting through the jail's office window. The light seemed as cold as the fresh snow that blanketed Cheyenne, as cold as the glare from Clay Stephens's eyes.

He was heavily shackled, his cuffed hands resting on the table before him. A light wool coat was thrown around his shoulders in deference to his position across the room from the potbellied stove.

He caught his reflection in the shaving mirror Stephens kept above the office's wash basin. Pale and sandy-haired, his complexion had lightened substantially in the past months of captivity, seeming to meld with the light tan, prison-issue shirt he wore. His moustache, usually carefully trimmed, seemed long and unruly, his hair bordering on shaggy. He had a week's growth of beard that itched to high heaven. His receding hairline seemed to unveil more wan forehead with each passing day. Even his light blue eyes seemed more washed out than usual. Not one taken to vanity, he nevertheless smiled grimly at the sight of what he'd become.

He was waiting for John Stain, and knew he'd continue waiting for the time being. Horn had dealt with Stain under other circumstances and found him to have the haughtiness of those who are customarily late, confusing it with intimidation.

Stephens sat in a wooden slat chair across the sparsely furnished office, a Winchester held loosely across his belly. He had stoked the fire within the stove and added several stumpy pine logs. November was cold in Wyoming, and the second storm of the season had just blown through the day before. As someone born and raised on the Gulf Coast of Texas, Stephens didn't like the cold. Not one bit.

He was not in a talkative mood and had merely led Horn to the table, sat him down, and retreated to the chair. He seemed to be mulling something over. A notorious back room gambler, Stephens never made an uncalculated move. Horn imagined he must be reckoning the personal odds Stain's visit might have on his position in life.

Sitting uncomfortably, Horn reflected on the events that had led to the meeting, events charged with arrogance and abandonment. He smiled at the thought of all the commotion his simple little note had caused.

He hadn't been sure the gambit would work, but, following his trial and murder conviction, his desperation had become overwhelming. His guilt over a checkered criminal career notwithstanding, he decided he did not want to die on a hangman's gallows, especially when his death would release so many others from their worldly obligations.

His first reaction had been to attempt to escape. He had done so, and had managed to get a short way out of town before being caught by the local populace and beaten to a pulp. At least twenty-five men had laid claim to recapturing the famous desperado.

Under the guise of writing letters to his brother in Colorado, Horn had outlined the complicity of members of the Wyoming Stock Growers Association in over a dozen murders. He gave dates and named names. And the biggest name of all was the former governor of the great state of Wyoming.

When he had finished his chronicle of death, he had entertained a visit from Hugh Carey, an old drinking partner, and had smuggled the journal to him. He then had written a letter to Governor Ford, given it to Stephens, and suggested that it should be delivered promptly. Stephens had looked at him questioningly, and then looked at the paper in his hands. The color had drained from the sheriff's face as he read the note.

The Hon. Ex-Gov. Ford,

Due to the unfortunate situation in which I am now engaged I find it necessary to convey that information concerning certain deaths of sheepmen and rustlers is now in the hands of trusted sources. Although I have led a cowardly life of sin I need more time to attain salvation than the hangman will allow. The evidence will be delivered to the U.S. Attorney in Denver immediately following my death. Were I you I'd wish me a long prosperous life.

Sincerely yours
Tom Horn

"This true?" Stephens had asked, looking up from the note.

"True as the risen Lord," had replied Horn laconically.

The sheriff had stared at Horn for a long moment, then had said: "Hmm. I got to figure out what to do, then, don't I?"

Now, three days later, Horn sat staring at the jail's front door, waiting to meet with the governor's emissary.

At 10:30 the door opened, and John Stain walked into the room. One of the West's wealthiest cattlemen, he radiated the assurance of a man used to power. He was a fastidious personality, impeccably groomed and soft-spoken. He wore a thick canvas overcoat and barely broken-in silverbelly beaver hat with a cattleman's crown. Beneath his coat, his black broadcloth suit was freshly brushed, with the starched white shirt contrasting with his dark mustachioed face.

"Sheriff Stephens," he said in greeting.

"Howdy, John," Stephens answered.

"The governor has requested that you stay while I interview Mister Horn. He values your counsel."

Stephens nodded his assent, but remained seated across the room.

Stain walked to the table where Horn waited, removed his coat and hat, and sat down facing him. He looked like some lavish bird, Horn thought, about to cluck and preen his feathers.

"Well, Tom, let's start talking," he said.

Horn mulled the command over for a moment, then said: "I'm not here to talk, Stain. I'm here to listen."

Stain's eyes bored into him, lowering only when Horn returned the gaze with an intensity few living men had experienced. The prisoner realized with some satisfaction that Stain—vainglorious, powerful Stain—was cowed when looking into the eyes of a killer.

"Well, what can I say?" Stain said softly. "You've caused one hell of a ruckus. I believe you told Governor Ford and myself after your trial that you would carry this, this *information,* to the grave. You weren't a blackmailer, I believe you said."

Horn chuckled and said cynically: "That was before I got to figuring that the grave is a mighty cramped place."

Stain gave a wry smile and said: "You hadn't thought of that before? You've put so many there."

The rage rose up in Horn, turning his face crimson. He fought for control, and said: "What I've done is done. Like as not, I'd change it if I could. There's nothing more to say. Now, there's not much time 'fore the lynching party the good people of Cheyenne have got planned. What are you gonna do to get me outta here?"

Stain stared at Horn, then shook his head slowly, adopting the demeanor of a banker denying a loan.

"I don't know, Tom. Maybe, if you hadn't killed that boy. . . ."

Through clenched teeth, Horn answered: "It's said that he was dressed like his papa. The same sheep-herding papa you and about a half dozen others, including the good ex-governor, hired me to shoot until he was dead."

Stain paused, then punctuated his words by tapping the desk top with a closed fist.

"Some acts are necessary, and some fall beyond the bounds of civilized action, Tom. Although you met with the governor, no specific actions were agreed upon. You and he, to the best of my recollection, were just talking some sort of speculation."

"Don't try to bullshit a bullshitter, Stain. Oh, I remember the conversation all right. You mentioned the target. I mentioned my fee. Everybody went away happy."

"Oh, to the contrary, Tom," said Stain. "I remember nothing about any killing. Especially of a boy. What was he, fourteen years old, Tom?"

Horn exhaled slowly. "Yeah, fourteen. That's what they say. They also say the bullets came from a Thirty-Thirty like my rifle. If that's true, Stain, you and Ford and them others pulled the trigger, big as life. At least that's what the U.S. Attorney's gonna say before twelve of your peers."

Stain kept his composure, obviously mulling over his response. Finally, with a touch of cynicism, he asked: "So, you're prepared to indict John Coble, also?"

Horn winced perceptibly at the mention of his friend and benefactor. He had told Coble of the plan during a visit two days earlier, making sure to watch the man's expressive eyes. Coble had listened, nodded, and assented. "I've left John Coble out of this," he said. "So will you."

Stain leaned back in his chair and thought for a moment. He looked around at Stephens.

"Sheriff, I assure you that Horn's accusations bear no fruit. They are completely without merit. However, the ex-governor is in a precarious situation. Of course, he has made political enemies who would love to see his downfall. As you know, others including myself feel he has greater things in store for him. Also, I would not like to see Governor Chatterton have to deal with potential political upheaval so early in his term.

"Now, the memory of the calamity in Johnson County is still fresh, and Governor Ford's connection with the Stock Growers Association is well known. The newspapers are clambering for not only Horn's head, but those of his supposed benefactors, as well. So, we have a problem. How can we solve it, gentlemen?"

Stephens stood and walked across the office, not answering. He stared at himself in the mirror for a moment, and turned to the men seated at the table. "You oughta be relieved, Tom," he said wryly. "Looks like the stock growers wanna make ya a deal."

Stain stared uncomfortably at his hands. He started to say something, but then caught himself.

Stephens crossed his arms and looked out the window into the street. With great finality, he said: "There's no way that we can stop the hangin'."

Horn laughed out loud and slammed his fists on the table, the metal handcuffs digging into the wood. He bellowed: "Then, by God, the good governor and Mister Stain here will be hanging on either side of me!"

Stain began to sputter and stood up, shouting incoherently.

"Hold on a minute!" yelled the sheriff, stopping Stain's outburst. "I said there'd be a hangin'. The people are too riled up to stop it now. Nope, Tom, we'll have to hang you." He looked directly into Horn's eyes, and let a sardonic smile transform his face, an idea forming across his features. "We just mebbe won't hafta kill you."

Chapter Three

His eyes followed the great crack across the cell's roughly plastered ceiling, traveling from the cobwebbed corner nearest the door's threshold three or four feet until it dissolved into dozens of smaller tributaries. The small cracks fanned out through the dingy plaster, with one taking a particular dogleg turn before reaching for the opposite wall.

The cracks had taken on a sense of drama to Horn, becoming a small world subject to the rule of light. In the morning, the dawn's first rays entering the window caused long shadows to intercept the cracks on the ravaged ceiling, creating a series of elongated canals. As the light brightened and flooded sections of the cell, the ceiling took on the flat, dusty aspect of the Army maps Horn had spent years perusing. The stains and discolorations had become various strata, and he'd turned the great crack into the Missouri River with its hundreds of tributaries fanning out into the vast reaches of the American West. The doglegged crack became the North Platte, leading ever westward, through Nebraska and directly to the heart of Wyoming, directly to the despoiled body of young Willie Nickell.

Over the past year boredom and frustration had caused Horn to commit the crooked paths of the cracks to memory. He felt himself to be a man of destiny and had seen great meaning in the smallest of his actions over the years. Now, occupying a tiny cot in a filthy jail cell, he had come to associate his life's landmarks with the rivers he had traveled. The meaning of his life became intertwined with a map created by cheap plaster, unkilned wood, and shoddy workmanship.

Lying on his back, breathing lightly and with expectation, he used the fissures as markers to remember the ebb and flow of his life, to try to make sense of the path that led to a filthy cot in a bug-infested, freezing Wyoming jail cell. A path that led to the gallows.

His road to the hangman figuratively began in the cell's corner, on the banks of the powerful Missouri River. As he stared at the fissures, he examined his beginnings, taking some strange comfort from the concentration that the recall of events forced him to undertake.

Most of all, he thought, he remembered the stories of Jesse and Frank. From his birth, Horn had seemed destined to fulfill his border state legacy. Growing up during Reconstruction, he and his peers were regaled by stories of Missouri's famous outlaws. The murderous James boys and their equally vile cousins, the Youngers, were, through some perverse turn of human nature, considered heroes by most who lived along the river. Boys growing up in Missouri's heat and humidity were titillated with tales of daring and come-uppance, always featuring Frank and Jesse liberating huge amounts of money from Yankees who deserved to be gut shot and left to die in the sun. If the outlaws murdered a few of the rich Eastern industrialists they robbed, so be it. It was divine retribution, all right. No one served God's fiery wrath more devoutly than the James Gang, and no one had bought into their legend more than young Tom Horn.

Young Horn spent every available minute daydreaming, placing himself in the rôle of the daring Jesse. He was often

31

startled when he emerged from such reverie, finding himself far from home with hours lost.

When his mother asked him about his long silences, he answered that he was only playing games in his head. She would look at him with her stern, Calvinist countenance, and her disdain would plainly show.

Martha Horn had been born in a dilapidated shack on the banks of the Ohio River, the fifth child and only girl of ten siblings. At thirteen, she had endured enough of both her father's fists and his lechery. She stowed away in the wagon of a traveling preacher and his entourage. When the girl was discovered, the Reverend Levi Kartz looked her over, knitted his eyebrows in prayer, and promptly raped her. She remained his concubine for four years, traveling with his small band throughout the country, following the great rivers from town to town. While recovering from her third miscarriage, Martha was left at a cheap boarding house in St. Louis with strict orders never to approach the preacher again under pain of eternal damnation.

Although Kartz left her with nothing in the way of earthly goods, he did manage to instill a genuine fear of God into her that would last her entire life. He also managed to teach her to read and write in order to transcribe his lengthy sermons.

Abandoned by Kartz, her prayers became rites of appeasement for her shortcomings, and her dearest hope was that the hell she was damned to inhabit would not be as terrible as she imagined.

Five years later, following a series of common law marriages that served only to keep food in her stomach, she entered into yet another with a raw-boned, foul-tempered ex-soldier named Trev Horn. They settled on a small farm near the Missouri town of Shawcroft where, to Martha's surprise and dread in light of her checkered yet childless past, she became extremely fertile. Four children were born in the space of six years, the last being a young dreamer named Thomas. Her pregnancy was agonizing, and she refused to have anything to do with the boy for the first two days of his life. Her husband grew tired of the squalling, hungry baby and beat Martha unmercifully, promising more if she didn't deal with the child. Broken and bloody, she picked up the baby and nursed it.

Over the next fourteen years, Martha continually prayed for God's forgiveness because of her apathy toward young Tom, her eyes tightly shut and her wrinkled forehead so screwed up in concentration that she received terrible headaches. When the pain began to be unbearable, she had little recourse but to blame her aimless son and to berate him in the process.

Nevertheless, he continued his "games." Sometimes, as he walked through the woods toward the great river on some errand, he allowed the trees to become enemies, the bushes to become pursuing lawmen. He would dash behind cover and create huge mental gun battles, each of them ending with him pointing a pistol at a gray-bearded Yankee colonel, laughing in his terrified face as he slowly squeezed the trigger.

With the birth of each of her children, Martha Horn grew increasingly distant from the physical world around her. She withdrew into the Good Book, reading in her slow, plodding manner and identifying prophecy in each of the holy verses. She distanced herself as much as possible from her boorish husband and embraced the word of God in the strict, unequivocal manner that had been ingrained by Levi Kartz. Aged well beyond her years, she knew she was past salvation, but she also could never stop trying to atone for her very existence.

Her older children kept their distance, sensing the dark and terrified core of their mother's soul. To this end, they sacrificed their little brother, formulating constant excuses to leave him with her. The young boy she despised became her only real companion, listening to her read from the Bible by the hour, watching her excitement as she divined some new meaning in a Scripture she'd read countless times.

For some reason even she could not fathom, she also taught the boy the rudimentary elements of reading and writing. Although ignored, he would not be illiterate.

The clapboard church three miles down the muddy road toward town became the center of their universe. Trev Horn would drop off Martha and Tom on his way into town in search of cheap whisky and soiled doves, and let them walk back, always the last to leave the small building, always engaging the stern minister in talk of hellfire and damnation.

Tom despised the church. He despised its people. He felt doomed and trapped each time they entered and encountered the flock of several dozen, each face more austere and unyielding than the last. His earliest memories were of the dour minister castigating the congregation for a wide variety of sins while his mother bowed her head and mumbled incomprehensible prayers.

As he grew, he came to know the church as a place of fear and dread, which was just fine with Martha. She ingrained the literal fear of God into her youngest son, constantly expounding on the essential nature of fright.

"You're to fear the Lord, your God, Thomas. Fear is a basic and useful emotion. If you don't fear, you will never attain salvation. You'll never love."

Despite his constant trepidation, he knew he must embrace the church with its fearsome and fearful people. If not, he would burn in eternal damnation, screaming in agony for eternity. His mother told him so.

It was in this church one summer Sunday that Tom received his first revelation. His mind had been wandering from his mother's teachings for some time, worrying about more pragmatic things, like his father's whippings and the James boys. Yet, on this day, the sermon seemed to hold more promise for the fourteen-year-old. Minister Dobbs had been talking for over two hours about God's law and the Almighty's plan for each individual life. He talked of the necessity to hold God within, no matter where the road might lead. Some divinely inspired intuition caused Tom to rouse himself from a state of near slumber and perk up his ears as Dobbs droned what was to become the ultimate truth in his life.

"Now, brothers and sisters," the preacher intoned, "we'll turn in God's Word to the Acts, Chapter Seventeen, beginning with Verse Twenty-Two. 'Then Paul stood in the midst of Mars hill and said . . . Ye men of Athens, I perceive that in all things ye are too superstitious.

" 'For as I passed by, and beheld your devotions, I found an altar with this inscription, To The Unknown God, Whom therefore ye ignorantly worship, him declare I unto you.

" 'God that made the world and all things therein, seeing that he is Lord of heaven and earth, dwelleth not in temples made with hands. . . .' "

Tom sat bolt upright, causing his mother to shoot him a venomous stare. He was completely oblivious to the preacher's continuing murmur. For the only time in his life, he locked eyes with his mother, forcing her to return her gaze to the Bible lying open on her lap. It was his first victory, made even more sweet by the absolute knowledge that had been imparted by the Scripture.

He was amazed by the passage. The great Apostle Paul, who spread the gospel of Jesus to the entire world, said that God didn't live in temples. Tom searched the small, shabby room with his eyes, realizing that its rough-cut timber and bone-jarring pews might not be God's home after all. His fear was a fear of people, not of God. If Paul could tell the Athenians that God wasn't at home in their beautiful stone temples, then He certainly didn't live in a cramped, gloomy wooden shack on the banks of the Missouri.

Sitting on a splinter-filled plank pew, Tom Horn lost his fear, not only of God, but of life as well. Decades later, he would realize that his mother had been right. When his fear of the Almighty dissipated, so, too, did his love. But for now, he was set free.

Walking back from church that afternoon, Tom allowed himself to look at the world in a different fashion. Like a just-released prisoner, he seemed to see things for the first time. The sickly sweet smell of the river coated his nostrils, and he drank in the summer humidity. The swarms of gnats seemed interesting rather than annoying. He saw the stunning green panorama before him as his own, with each majestic tree placed along the worn path by God expressly for the enjoyment of passers-by, expressly for *him*.

The spell was broken by his mother's lifeless voice.

"You are to have Acts Nineteen memorized for Wednesday service," she sighed as they walked. "We may as well begin. Repeat after me . . . 'And it came to pass, that, while Apollos was at Corinth. . . .' "

"No."

Martha's head instantly snapped toward her son, her face a mask of disbelief. Her eyes bored into his as she grabbed his arm and hissed: "You will *not* talk to me in such a manner. *Ever*."

The boy returned his mother's stare, his demeanor equally obstinate. Haltingly he said: "I'll talk to you how I want."

He saw her arm swinging toward his face and with lightning quick reflexes caught it by the wrist. He squeezed as hard as he could, forcing the arm to her side. He held her there, compelling her to stand and listen.

"I'm through with church, too," he said. He looked quickly around, and his free arm made an arc encompassing the river, the forest, the entire world. "From now on *this* is my church, and there ain't nothin' you can do about it."

He thrust his mother's arm away, nearly knocking her to the ground, and was off like a shot through the hardwood forest, toward the river. He thought the exhilarating, uplifting emotion that filled his heart must be identical to that the James and Younger boys had felt when they knocked off a Yankee bank.

He ran as hard and as long as he could, expending energy that had been pent up forever in his soul. He trod moss-covered paths in tunnels of impossibly green foliage, knowing *exactly* where he was going, where he would end up. Now, he knew, he was free. He could follow the river or go west to the high mountains. No one could stop him. No one would dare.

Worn out, he stopped and sat under an elm on a bluff a couple of hundred yards away from the riverbank. He knew that he would have to go home and face his hysterical mother. Of course, that meant that he would be beaten by his father. But all things considered, he could take the demeaning mistreatment until his plan for leaving was in place. He would scheme carefully, he thought, and grab the world that was now his.

Chapter Four

It was nearly two more years before his escape came about. Slowly his mother had withdrawn into herself, speaking infrequently to her husband and older children, and never to Tom. She began making candles from the tallow of animals killed by her husband and sons, and burning them late into the night, murmuring passages from her worn Bible as the flames' dim reflection danced across the pages. She became bone thin, forgetting to eat and forgetting to feed her family, all the time perusing the Holy Book. She put up with her husband's beatings and recriminations, regarding them as mere annoying interludes between her quest for the Scriptures' ultimate truth. She barely noticed the broken wrist and cracked ribs, and her only request of her husband was that he drive her to church services on his way to Shawcroft's bars and bordellos.

Tom's two older sisters had taken up with laborers from St. Louis, and his brother was rarely around. That left him virtually alone in the world, caught between a mother bordering on insanity and a father steeped in bitter self-loathing. He walked a delicate line between them, doing his best to stay invisible, unnoticed.

Tom had grown tall and lanky, with the deceptive strength of raw-boned boys. At nearly 6'3", he was taller than his father and towered over most of the other boys his age. He did virtually all the work around his family's tiny, dilapidated farm, preparing the ground for seed and keeping the weeds cut back to an acceptable level. He became an expert with a rifle, putting 'possum, squirrel, and rabbit on the family's table. To waste ammunition was to invite his father's fists, so by his sixteenth birthday his aim was straight and true. Not a varmint along the great river was safe from his keen eye.

He also tended the family's two horses, one an ancient mare on her last legs, the other a serviceable gelding Tom's father had won in a poker game. Tom Horn became a familiar sight in the adjacent counties, riding the dun gelding as smooth as an eagle on the breeze.

It was the gelding that eventually caused it, caused him to run and to keep running. His father's gelding.

Trevor Horn was a horseman. His first memories were of the horses at his father's livery stable in rural Illinois. Throughout his life he could recall the stable with vivid clarity—the dusty smell of hay mixed with that of horses' pungent urine, the smooth leather of the tack hung in the long polished rack against the outer wall, and even the deep laughter of riders who brought their mounts to be stabled and shared a quick pull from his father's gallon jug of corn mash.

By the time he was five, he was an accomplished rider, often accompanying his father into the thick deciduous forests in search of deer. His father doted on him, calling him Trev-boy. He took his young sidekick with him wherever he went. Most people in the county called them "Big" and "Little" and were amazed at the man's dedication to son. In young Trev's eyes, the sun rose and set according to his father's whims.

He was with his father on one of their so-called venison

runs when the elder Horn laid his rifle against a sapling before jumping over a small stream. As he sprang, his long coat caught a branch, knocking the rifle onto a waist-high jumble of cracked boulders and discharging it. He was in mid-air when the rifle's ball ripped into his back and exited through his neck. As his body flipped in mid-air, he caught a glimpse of the deep blue sky and took comfort in its beauty.

He landed face up in the shallow creek and died minutes later while ten-year-old Trev raced back to the stable for help. His body was found a few feet downstream, moved slowly by the water's faint power. Tiny minnows fed on the precious blood that flowed from his wounds, and his hair swirled around his head in the current. Those in the party who retrieved his body were surprised at the serene countenance he wore to face eternity. They questioned how such a violent death could result in the calm they saw in his face. Had he been alive, he would have told them. His last thoughts were of his boy—his boy and the azure sky.

Trev's mother was devastated at her husband's death and took to wearing black around the clock. In the first few months after the accident she became a local mystery, her black-veiled personage seen only at Sunday services. It was rumored that unearthly wailing was heard from the house, should one venture to walk by in the late evening.

Yet, despite her well-publicized grief, over the next couple of years she became the object of desire for several well-to-do suitors. Little by little, the veils were lifted and the wailing ceased. The black dresses were soon packed in a seaman's chest, and, by the time Trev was thirteen, he lived in a large house in Grenville with his mother and stepfather. Within two years, he had a new baby sister. He was dressed in gabardine and broadcloth and was sent to a private school where he read the classics while dreaming of tracking deer in the cool autumn breeze.

He hated his life. He considered his mother a traitor and his stepfather a passionless boor. He dreamed constantly of his father and consistently woke up screaming and crying from unimaginably horrid dreams.

He began skipping school and stealing whisky from the leaded glass cabinet in the parlor. After he pushed his instructor over a desk, rather than be bullied into admitting that his last name was now Saunders, his stepfather took a shaving strop and beat him unmercifully, drawing welts and blood all over his body. During his recovery, his mother never once stepped through the door to his room. He could hear her cooing and singing to his little sister in the next room, her voice lilting and gay.

At sixteen, Trev responded to the constant flirtations of a merchant's daughter named Sarah Price. Sneaking into a shed in back of her father's shop, they proceeded to kiss and touch until his kisses became bruising, his touches malicious. She began to strike at him and tried to call for help. Before he beat her unconscious, the last thing she thought was that she was staring into the eyes of the devil himself.

Hours later the town constable came to the Saunders' house and advised Trev's livid parents of their son's activities. As they were an influential family, he accepted generous stipends for both himself and the Price girl and left the matter of punishment in Trev's stepfather's hands. Before he was out of earshot, he heard the lashes of the strop and the screams of the boy.

Three days later, barely able to move, Trevor Horn slipped out of the house with a carpetbag filled with clothes and four $50 gold pieces stolen from his stepfather. He painfully saddled an old mare that had been bred by his father and trotted off toward the west. No one followed.

Over the next few years, he worked his way west, breaking horses for the Army and laboring on the docks of St. Louis. He found he loved the taste of whisky and the fast life of the town's notorious bars. He became a proficient gambler and for a brief time even owned a roadhouse. He drank up any small profit and soon found himself accepting a token payment from a St. Joseph horse breeder, Captain Cleveland Howard. The breeder now owned the bar and kept Horn on as both bartender and stable master.

On a trip to the East to buy horseflesh for Howard, Horn couldn't resist the temptation to swing back through the place of his birth. He stopped at the spot where his father had been killed, sitting on a rotting stump and staring into the cold trickle of water. Although the site looked identical to the way it had the day his father died, something seemed different, almost peculiar. The soft, rotting humus on the forest's floor seemed to hold mysteries that could be dug up if only he had the time and the will. The elms and willows had stories to tell, if only he would listen.

He mulled the strange emotion for an entire afternoon, but was unable to do much more than occasionally catch a mental whiff of something he thought to be very important. Finally he rose stiffly, mounted his horse, and took off for Grenville. He skirted the village, riding up a side street in the twilight. He cautiously slipped up the street where his mother lived and made his way toward the house of his stepfather. As he neared, he became confused, feeling eerily out of place. The two-story brick house was gone, with another much smaller frame house built on the same lot.

He quickly reined his horse in and retreated to a roadhouse on the main street that had not been in business when he had fled. After tying the horse to a post outside, he cautiously entered the tavern. He ordered whisky and engaged the barkeep in conversation, asking about the potential for buying horses in the county.

He remarked offhandedly that he was from the area but hadn't been around for a while. What had happened to the great brick house two blocks over? The barkeep raised his eyebrows and allowed that he thought everyone had heard about the fire. It had been started six or seven years ago by a little baby girl a year or so old who had pulled an oil lamp off a table. The baby's father was trapped inside the house and died with the infant in his arms. The mother managed to escape by jumping through a window. She was inconsolable after, screaming and calling for her baby and for her teenage son who had disappeared a few weeks earlier. Her neighbors took her in, but a couple of weeks after the fire her body was found out in the woods by a creek where her first husband had died in a freak accident. She'd put a pistol to her temple and squeezed the trigger.

Trev Horn stopped the shaking of his hands by downing another shot of whisky. He then ordered a full bottle, threw a coin on the bar, and took off into the night.

After spending two days blind drunk in a cornfield north of the village, Horn rode directly to the town of Springfield, where he sent a letter to his employer, arranging for the delivery of the horses he had purchased. He then enlisted in the Army, hoping to stay one step ahead of his family's ghastly lament.

The next three years were spent on the Western plains, at outposts even a scorpion would find uninhabitable. At times he thought he'd become part of the interminable high desert and knew he'd always carry the sound of the ever-present wind in deepest corners of his being.

Those years served as a panacea for Trev Horn's soul,

and he found he was afraid of very little. Although his ghosts were laid to rest, his taste for whisky and gambling grew, and, when he stabbed a sergeant during a drunken brawl, he grabbed the first horse he could find and headed east.

He returned to St. Louis only to find that his former employer, Howard, had closed the bar, saddled up his horses, and moved back to St. Joseph. He went back to work on the docks. Although the work was backbreaking, he still managed to spend most of his nights in any of a dozen rollicking taverns. It was in one of these, The Hind, that he met a thin young woman who called herself Martha Kartz. He'd never seen a woman in a tavern before. Intrigued, he offered to buy her a drink. She refused, saying her stomach couldn't bear whisky. She would, however, bear Trev Horn four children over the next few years.

He managed to scrape up enough cash in a series of faro games to buy a small farm near the town of Shawcroft. He had always imagined himself as a gentleman farmer of sorts, growing a few crops while dabbling in horses. He thought the small farm would have to do for the time being.

When it came time to take possession of the property, he threw all the belongings he owned into a trunk in the corner of a room he and Martha shared. It was only when he told her he was leaving that Martha stared at him for a moment, then began reading her Bible aloud. Not knowing what else to do, he led her outside and sat her on a buckboard. They made the trip, after which he ensconced her in a two-room shack on the property before taking off to experience the nightlife of the small town.

A few weeks later, in the midst of a drunken binge, he suddenly realized that he wished he had never met her. In fact, he despised her. Her constant reading of the Bible was eerie to him, and he had quickly found that she viewed the world as much more of a quagmire than he did. Even her sexuality she perceived as a punishment, a type of self-flagellation aimed at atonement for her very life.

One besotted night after she had given birth to their first son, he reached to caress her as she stood inside the building's doorway only to have her pull away. He immediately struck her, sending her across the room and into a wall. She barely missed overturning a lamp that, he realized, would likely have resulted in the same fiery fate that had killed his little sister. He walked to Martha, picked her up, and hit her again as punishment. He would never know that she looked into the same fiery eyes first glimpsed in Illinois by young Sarah Price.

To his amazement and initial shame, he found that he liked hitting her and, as soon as the children began to grow, that he liked hitting them. He would spend as little time as possible tending the farm and as much as possible drinking corn whisky and cheaply brewed ale. Under the influence, he would often weep for love of his children, only to beat them unmercifully when he got home.

Over the years, his habits became more extreme and his fists quicker toward his family. Especially to his youngest, Tom. At sixteen, there was something about the boy that bothered Trev. Perhaps it was his general ability. The boy could do just about anything with little prodding. He took to horses even quicker than Trev had and was a better farmer by the time he was twelve. He could shoot as well as anyone in the county and was starting to draw the attention of local farm girls, farm girls Trev felt should be interested in more mature men of the world. Although Trev had tattooed the boy with his knuckles over the years, Tom still had spirit and had stopped the beating of his mother several times, taking the brunt of his father's assaults himself. In his lucid moments Trev was actually amazed at how the pitiful woman could still manage to hate her son so much when he was her only protector. But then he couldn't understand why she had taught him to read, or why she emotionally abandoned him after his religious rebellion.

When they talked, it was only of the James Gang or of putting meat on the table. With Tom around, Trev had little to do but drink and gamble. He became very good at both.

He won the gelding in a day-long faro contest, accepting the horse in trade for a hundred-dollar debt from the son of an Army colonel. He took great satisfaction in the irony that the military was still a part of his life, supplying a deserter with horseflesh.

He was sitting in the tavern on a Saturday afternoon, engaged in a drunken, foul-tempered game, when he folded his cards and went to the bar for a drink. He walked up to the bar, little more than a plank set across two cross braces, and ordered whisky from the sweating bartender. He stood next to Amos Whitney, a blacksmith who spent more time shooting back rotgut than forging horseshoes. Huge sweat stains down the sides of his shirt and a three-days' growth of beard belied the binge he was undertaking.

Whitney nodded at Horn. "Howdy, Trev," he said.

"Amos," Horn answered. He sighed heavily and shook his head.

"Havin' trouble today?" asked Whitney.

"Lady luck does seem to have flown, Amos," Horn answered. "I 'spect I'd best head back out to the place, get that lazy kid of mine to workin'."

Whitney chuckled and said: "I seen that boy o' yorn t'other day, Trev. Week or so ago. He rides like the wind, he shore do."

"What?" said Horn, surprised.

"Yeah, he was racin' that geldin' o' yers down along Blue Creek, givin' it its head, awright. Yup, that boy can ride."

Horn looked down into his glass and squinted. The last thing he wanted in this place was to hear what a fine rider his boy was. "Well, he'd best not be ridin' my hoss, that's fer sure. If he ain't huntin', he best not be ridin', I say."

Horn turned and headed for the door. Outside, he stopped and took a deep breath, letting his eyes adjust to the light. He then walked unsteadily to the rickety stable down the street and retrieved his old mare. As he rode home, he began to stew about Whitney's comments.

"God-damn' kid better be out huntin' varmints, 'stead o' racin' hosses," he mumbled to himself. "Only god-damn' good hoss I got, and the god-damn' kid's out running it. Prob'ly bust its leg or sumpin', then what've I got? God-damn' nothin', thas what."

The mare knew its way home down the country lane and turned into the short path leading to the house without the benefit of Horn's guidance. It made its way directly to a small shack that passed for a barn and stopped before the closed door.

Horn was still seething and had decided to find Tom and work him over a bit, teach him a fine lesson. He was in luck. He could hear his son at work in the barn, and lumbered off the mare. He opened the door to see Tom removing a bridle from the gelding. The boy had obviously been riding and was beginning to brush the lightly lathered animal. Tom turned at his father's entrance and nodded, returning to work on the horse's mane.

Without a word, Horn strode unsteadily to the boy and threw a powerful punch at his head. Tom's reflexes overcame his surprise, and he quickly pulled back, receiving only a glancing blow. He looked in disbelief at his father, who was now coming after him with eyes burning.

"You god-damn' pup," he sputtered. "I told you that hoss is *mine!* You ain't gonna be out prancin' him around the county none. Not where my friends can see an' come tell me about my boy running this hoss into the ground! I'm gonna whup you till you cain't walk, boy!"

Horn threw another punch at Tom, which landed on his shoulder, spinning him around. The boy tripped over a slat and landed flat on his back, causing dirt, manure, and hay from the filthy floor to explode up and around him. The airborne dust caused him to sneeze violently, and, when he looked back up, his father was standing ten feet away, feverishly chewing his lip, almost frothing at the mouth.

At that moment Tom suddenly was overcome with an ice cold, absolute calm. He looked up at the man who had inspired fear so often, and felt nothing but abhorrence. In an instant he knew it was time, time for his life to begin.

"Get up, boy!" Horn roared. "I'll teach you to mess with my hoss!"

Tom quickly stood and stretched to his full height, looking down on his father. He locked into the man's eyes, sensing their fire and fury, and returned the stare with rage of his own. Slowly, without breaking the stare, he leaned down and grabbed the slat he had tripped over. His father began to approach.

"Don't you dare, boy!" he yelled just as Tom swung from the floor, putting all his weight into the weapon he held. The flat of the splintery board struck Trev Horn directly on the side of his head, shattering his eardrum and lacerating his cheek. The man slipped in a pile of manure and fell back to the floor, clutching his head and moaning.

He tried to rise, but Tom was on him, kicking and punching, biting and gouging. Like a whirlwind, he attacked his father with no thought of direction, only of destruction.

Horn tried to rise, but Tom quickly stood and kicked him under the chin, opening a frightful wound. Horn spewed the contents of his stomach over one of the rough plank walls from a kick in the abdomen and lost consciousness when Tom kicked him in the groin.

An entire lifetime of being constantly beaten and debased spilled out of young Tom Horn, and he would think, later, he may have enjoyed his revenge too much. But now nothing pleased him more than seeing Trev Horn's lying prostrate on the dirt floor of the barn, unconscious in his own vomit and blood.

Spent, Tom stood unsteadily over the disabled form of his father. Catching his breath, he reached down and grabbed the man by the front of his shirt, pulling him into a sitting position. The stench was almost unbearable, but he lightly tapped his father's cheeks until the fluttering eyes seemed to indicate a return to consciousness.

"Pa?" he questioned flatly between ragged breaths.

Horn slowly opened his eyes, not seeming to believe where he was. His eyes focused on his son. Tom grabbed the shirt tighter and pulled Horn's face to within inches of his. The stinking breath and battered flesh were almost more than he could bear, but retribution was at hand, and not even the dogs of hell could stop him now.

"You beat me for the last time, Pa," he said in a staccato whisper. "Now . . . I'm bigger 'n you, I'm stronger 'n you, and I'm one hell of a lot smarter 'n you. So, I figger that rather than spend any more time around here punchin' on you, I'd best be off."

He sighed and watched Trev Horn's wounded face, wondering if the man was attempting to understand. He finally decided it didn't matter.

"I thought about killin' ya right here," he said. "I don't suppose I will, 'cause then they'd prob'ly come after me. But you should know, *Pa*"—he spat out the word—"that I would love to do it. I'd *love* to!" he shouted as he threw Horn back down to the floor, causing his head to bounce with a hollow thud on the packed dirt.

Tom grabbed a hemp sack, walked out of the barn and to the house. He slammed open the door, startling his mother. She almost dropped the open Bible lying in her lap, catching it as it slid off her knees. She frantically turned the pages to find her place, not looking up at Tom as he walked directly to his cot and tossed his few belongings into the bag. He threw on his heavy woolen coat and jammed his rabbit-felt hat down low on his head. He grabbed the Winchester from the corner and turned to see his mother sitting erectly, silently mouthing Scripture, ignoring him as always. He stopped for a second in front of her, then quickly walked past her and out the door.

He saddled the gelding, taking his time to make sure the harness and straps would not hurt the animal during the long upcoming ride. He knotted the sack and attached it to the back of the saddle, adjusting it so it wouldn't rub the horse's rump, causing an abrasion. He then strapped the sheathed rifle to the saddle, walked the gelding out of the barn, and mounted.

He stopped and stared at the house he had called his home and despite himself felt some deep sadness at his departure. Fear gripped him momentarily, and all he could see ahead was a future of death and destruction. Shaking his head violently, he jumped off the horse and strode into the barn, stopping before his father.

Tom watched as Trev Horn groaned and tried to move. The noises he made were disgusting, and Tom nearly allowed himself to feel pity. The thousands of emotions that ran through him pulled him in every direction at once, clouding his mind and confusing his very soul. He found himself looking at the plank ceiling and then down again at his father's form.

He stood above his father for a long minute, until the man opened one eye and looked up. The absolute hate in that gaze was palpable, and Tom could feel it burn into his brain.

Tom stared back and started to say something. Horn groaned once again, a broken, phlegm-filled sound that served to mock the boy's sensibilities. Finally Tom shook his head and, losing his last vestige of control, delivered one more savage kick to his father's ribs. The crack was audible, like a dry stick being snapped.

The last time Tom would ever see his father, Trev Horn was writhing in agony on the hard-packed dirt floor, more of an animal than the rodents who hid in the barn's dark corners. It seemed appropriate, Tom thought.

Two loud explosions on the street outside the jail jolted Tom Horn from his reverie. He jumped up to the barred window and wiped the fogged glass with his hand, expecting to see gun play of some sort below. Instead, he gazed through the thick glass and watched a distorted automobile crawl down the snow-covered street, belching black smoke and occasionally backfiring with the sound of a pistol shot.

He sighed and returned to the cot, stretching out on the scratchy woolen blanket and trying to recapture the quarter-century old ghosts he had resurrected. Once again he focused on the cracked ceiling, willing his mind to travel the years from Missouri to Wyoming, from the ugly past to the deadly present. But it was no use. He couldn't recreate the time and place, and he found he didn't really want to recall that early life on the Missouri.

Lying there, he heard a faint noise, a deep drone of sorts. A voice perhaps. Yes. A voice with familiar tones followed by nearing footsteps.

He sat up carefully on the edge of his bunk, and then rose silently, facing the door. Finally the footsteps stopped, and Clay Stephens's voice drifted through from the outside.

"Visitor, Tom."

"Yeah, I know," Horn said to himself.

The lock was undone, and the door slowly opened. A stocky man with a full moustache and black beaver-felt hat of the type favored by cattlemen entered and stopped. He carried a heavy wool coat with a sheepskin collar over his arm, soft buckskin gloves protruding from one of the pockets. Dark stubble dotted the neck and chin that emerged from a frayed but newly starched collar. He stared for a moment at Horn with world-weary eyes, then smiled and walked forward to shake the prisoner's hand.

"I'm here with news," said John Coble.

Chapter Five

Over the weeks since his trial and conviction, Horn felt like a hive of bees had invaded his brain. He was incapable of making rational decisions, or of even thinking straight. He was overwhelmed by a constant hubbub, the buzzing of a million circumstances—the terror of what would be and the lost promise of what might have been.

His waking moments were characterized by an absolute inability to think beyond the next moment, and in the process stopping any true function, any capacity to plan or visualize the future. His dreams were one-on-one sessions with young Willie Nickell, the boy standing on the fresh-cut timber of a massive gallows, holding a knotted noose while favoring Horn with a grin straight from hell.

Sometimes the boy's grievous wounds were in evidence, and sometimes not. Strangely the dreaming Horn felt ill at ease when the boy seemed whole. He felt as if there was something he could do to stop Willie's killing.

He memorized the bricks, wood, and plaster of his cell, and moved around the tiny space with the assurance of a ruler in his domain. He found himself becoming nocturnal, relishing the dark nights before resting in the predawn. As the days progressed, he began to think he knew what it was like to be blind, having actually to sense objects through touch and echoes in the darkness. During the day he found himself anxiously awaiting the coming night. He reasoned that tackling the variables of this new dim domain was the only thing that kept him sane.

His hearing became incredibly acute. He could sense changes in the prison's structure as the seasons changed, as timbers settled and new mortar dried. He recognized individual voices from their mere timbre, often on the street as they stopped to talk before entering the building. He could identify the walk of each deputy and visitor as they approached his cell. He distinguished the faint sounds of other prisoners as they snored or wept or vomited or voided their bladders. Like a dog naturally cataloging each and every scent it ever encountered, Horn created a complex mental directory that served to mark and identify every aspect of his imprisonment. He realized this activity was absolutely useless, but it provided his only comfort.

Tall, thin, and wiry by nature, he became downright skinny, his ribs showing like a starving animal when he changed his shirt. He was a gaunt specter, awaiting the coming of his dark-cowled twin to lead him up the steps to a knotted rope and eternal damnation.

He was a man gradually giving up hope.

Yet a glimmer of faith did remain. His confrontation with John Stain and Clay Stephens the day before had given him food for thought. Stephens was putting together a plan, something that had to do with a charlatan's trick that would spring Horn from his imprisonment while somehow mollifying a vengeful public. As always, Stephens was quiet, playing his cards close to the vest. He would not respond to Horn's inquiries about his intentions, and he was equally obtuse when Stain questioned him. He had returned Horn to his cell and left with Stain. Horn stood at his cell's murky window and watched the two indistinct, blurry figures below walk down the icy boardwalk, off toward the west, toward Ford's office, he presumed.

And now, his friend and protector stood in the cell, telling him there was news. Good news or bad news, Horn wondered.

"Well, John, news is a fine thing, all right," Horn said wryly. "I just hope it's news of a suitable nature."

The cattleman looked at Horn and smiled shyly, the crow's feet at the corners of his eyes deepening. "You know me, Tom," he said softly. "I never was one to stick my nose where it don't belong. I'm not a rumor monger, by God."

Both men chuckled nervously as Coble walked to Horn's cot and sat on the edge. The odors of wet felt and wool followed Coble, filling the cell. The cattleman took his hat off and set it crown down on the floor. His graying hair retained the permanent ring that resulted from a lifetime of wearing high-crowned felt hats. He ducked his head and ran his hand through the thinning hair, something he always did when either nervous or in deep thought.

For the hundredth time, Horn reflected that John Coble was not cut out for the cattle business. He detested the cutthroat tactics, the scheming, and the sometimes necessary use of force that were all part of raising cattle in the West. Of all the men involved in this nasty enterprise, himself included, Horn figured Coble was the only one who retained any semblance of moral values. He did his best to walk a straight line down a crooked road, and he did it better than anyone.

Yet even Coble held dark secrets and had frequent nightmares of his own. Always reluctant when it came to matters of force, he nonetheless understood the necessity of controlling Wyoming's vast range. It was imperative to the health of his industry, he thought, and to the future of the state.

The two had met as a result of a telegram delivered to Horn at a Denver saloon some years earlier. Horn had been standing at the bar, smoking a cigar and contemplating joining a game across the room when a Western Union courier walked in, spied him, and sullenly handed him the message.

He waited until the messenger turned and walked away before reading the dispatch. It was from someone named John Coble in Iron Mountain, Wyoming. He represented a group of Wyoming cattlemen, mostly members of the Stock Grower's Association, and he had heard of Horn.

As had many. In a time of increasing social organization, Tom Horn was building a reputation as an outsider, an anomaly. Apart from a few gunmen and outlaws still at large in the great, unpopulated areas of Wyoming and Montana, Horn was one of the few real-life throwbacks to the frontier of a few decades earlier. As a mere boy, he had ridden with the legendary scout Al Sieber throughout Arizona. He spoke Spanish and the Apache tongue. He had served as a deputy sheriff, Army scout, and, it was rumored, a bounty hunter.

Now he was something else entirely. He dubbed his new calling "stock detective," and he was known to be extremely effective in dealing with livestock rustlers. A year earlier, it was whispered, Horn had traveled to the Powder River country of Wyoming to deal with a problem. After he hooked up with Frank Canton, who worked for the Wyoming Stock Grower's Association, Ranger Jones was cut down by rifle fire. A few days later John Tisdale was found with an exit wound in his chest, the result of an excellently placed .30-30 slug fired from a hundred yards to the rear.

Earlier that spring, Horn had ostensibly shown up in Johnson County, Wyoming as one of the infamous Invaders. Although he wasn't present at the killing of Nate Champion and Nick Rae at Kaycee, his long-range shooting abilities were intimated to have ended the lives of other so-called rustlers in Johnson County.

When the populace in Wyoming grew weary of the goings on around Buffalo, he returned south, taking on odd jobs in Colorado, Arizona, and New Mexico. An excellent cowboy, he could always count on picking up pocket money from the growing amount of rodeo competitions springing up around the country. He was also a fixture at sharp-shooting competitions. More often than not, he walked away with the prize. At the same time he was garnering a reputation as someone to contact when a problem arose having to do with property disputes. The problems were generally taken care of.

His welcome began to be worn out in the Four Corners area, and he figured he'd try his luck in the West's Queen City—Denver. The town was growing by leaps and bounds even now, nearly four decades following the discovery of gold at the confluence of the South Platte River and Cherry Creek by a group of rag-tag miners from Georgia, most of them Cherokees. The flamboyant Georgian, William Green Russell, and his companions had stumbled on the perfect site for a town, an ideal setting at the end of the trail for those who would follow Horace Greeley's forthcoming advice and take off for the West. The wild and woolly days were over, but Denver was still a spirited town. Sometimes even old Bill Cody could be spied holding court in the taverns on Market Street when his Wild West Show was not touring Europe.

Horn could feel the stares that followed him on the streets of Denver and took great pleasure in being a man to deal with. However, being a burgeoning legend had its limitations. It got Horn credit at Denver's taverns, all right, but money was short. Horn grimly thought that he had inherited little of his father's ability at the gaming tables. He did, however, share Trev Horn's taste for whisky, and he spent much of his time recovering from nasty drunken binges. Finally he was broke.

He was forced to begin thinking about finding meaningful work. When Coble's telegram arrived, it proved fortuitous. The cattleman had asked Horn to consider meeting with a group of stock growers in the Cheyenne area to discuss the rampant rustling problem.

Horn neatly knocked back a shot of rotgut that had been aging on the bar and left the tavern. He walked two blocks to the Western Union station and wired John Coble at Iron Mountain, Wyoming.

Dressed in well-worn boots, denim trousers, a new waistcoat, and a short woolen jacket, he was on the next train to Cheyenne.

The meeting with the cattlemen was to be held in the smoking room of a well-appointed Cheyenne hotel. John Coble met Horn at the Union Pacific station and entertained him with small talk for a half hour or so on a mahogany bench in a dim corner. Eventually he stood and motioned to Horn. As they walked out of the station and onto the worn boardwalk, he told Horn about the myriad problems that existed in the area.

"Tom," he said, "it's obviously no mystery to you. I was asked to send for you by a committee of men who have interest in the livestock industry. When it comes right down to it, we're losing our spurs to rustlers. And that don't even count the range them squatters have their sheep eatin' up. No, it's a bad time to be raising cattle on this range, and we gotta do something about it."

Horn smiled and said nothing, preferring to let Coble come right out with it.

Coble continued. "We need someone like you, Tom. Someone to put the fear of God into these rascals. We've got Joe LeFors, of course, but he's spread out all over the north part of Wyoming and Montana. Don't know how much use he is, anyhow. And Canton . . . well, you know about Canton."

Horn raised his eyebrows, indicating that he did indeed know about Frank Canton. He was one of the few who knew the former Johnson County sheriff as Joe Horner, a mad dog murderer from Texas.

"So, we've all decided to meet and see if we can come to some agreement. Now, there's talk that gun play is necessary, but I hope it doesn't have to come to that. Most-uh these squatters are poor folk, seem pretty miserable to me. But them sheep breed like roaches, an' you've seen what they do to the range.

"Now, the rustlers, they're just small-time bullies who put their stake on the big livestock growers havin' more beef on the hoof than they can count. John Stain or Frank Webster ain't gonna miss a few head, they say. Well, they're wrong."

Coble paused, and the men stopped walking. He stood on the boardwalk and shuffled his feet slightly. Horn looked down and noticed that the black steer-hide boots were worn enough to be comfortable. No show here, he thought. The real thing, through and through. When he looked back up, Coble was staring directly at him, his mouth formed into a whimsical smile.

"I think a man with your reputation may serve to get some o' them boys thinkin' how life might be better in Utah or California," he said.

Horn smiled and, seeing the twinkle in Coble's eyes, actually laughed out loud. "Well, it beats crossin' the River Styx, don't it, Mister Coble?" he said.

The two men chuckled as Coble reached up to tug on his thick moustache.

"Mister Coble, I'll tell you what I think," Horn continued. "I think there's many ways of makin' your point without resortin' to bloodshed. But there's always someone who won't listen to reason, always someone who thinks your cattle belong to him, that your land belongs to him. There's other methods of persuasion that become necessary as circumstances dictate. Now, thievin' cattle is still a crime in these United States, if I'm not mistaken. People are supposed to pay for crime, least that's what I learned as a deputy sheriff down in Arizona. I don't think things have changed so much in the last few years to make that a rash statement."

Coble looked long and hard at Horn, causing him to shift his gaze. At length, Coble nodded his head almost imperceptibly and stuck out his hand.

"I believe the men we'll meet shortly will take to you, Tom. I think we can do business."

The two men grasped hands and shook powerfully. Coble disengaged and began leading Horn to the hotel. He stopped momentarily, looked at Horn, and smiled.

"Oh, and, Tom . . . call me John."

From that first meeting, the two men cemented a curious friendship. Coble certainly knew Horn's capabilities and did not approve of the extreme sanctions employed by the gunman. Yet he was drawn to Horn and genuinely liked him.

For his part, Horn sensed Coble's basic decency and over the course of their friendship adopted a protective attitude toward the cattleman. He didn't think Coble would shirk from doing what must be done, but at the same time he wanted to make sure Coble's more noble sensibilities won out when necessary. Coble would likely provide a good counterpoint to his rashness, a governor to his temper.

The two men walked across the road and into a spectacular Victorian parlor. The hotel's lobby was designed as a sitting room, with the desk set unobtrusively in the rear of the room. Comfortable furniture was situated around the room, and crystal chandeliers hung from the fifteen-foot stamped tin ceilings, giving it the look and feel of a ballroom.

Coble and Horn walked through the lobby toward a double door next to the desk. Coble nodded to a fat man in a brown suit who sat behind the desk. The man stood, his open jacket revealing the butt of a .45 Colt stuffed into his pocket, then opened the door for the two men. They entered into a good-size room appointed with rich oxblood leather furniture. A dozen men sat and stood around the room. They were in various stages of Western dress, from formal black broadcloth suits to rugged denim range wear. They obviously knew each other well, and their collective curiosity about seeing Horn was evident in their anxious demeanors.

A faint haze from cigar smoke hung about the ceiling, and the smell of strong black coffee permeated the room. The thick, woven carpet served to tone down the naturally bright acoustics of the cavernous room. This was a sanctum, Horn realized, and he removed his hat. He felt for a moment as if he had walked into a church for the first time in nearly thirty years.

Each of the men turned toward the door as Coble led Horn into the assembly and quietly began ushering him around the room. "Tom, this here's Peter Cooper of the Diamond C," he began.

Horn grasped Cooper's outstretched hand and noted that this was a man who actually worked his spread. The sun-weathered skin and deep crow's feet attested to his range worthiness, as did the white forehead that was obviously hidden from the sun by a broad-brimmed hat when out working livestock. Cooper and Horn engaged in momentary small talk, then Coble gently put a hand on Horn's shoulder and moved him on.

Each of the cattlemen waited their turn as Horn was individually introduced and shook each hand around the room. The introductions over, Coble asked Horn to take a seat on an empty leather divan. He reached into a humidor, sitting on a carved mahogany table, and removed two cigars. Handing one to Horn, he sat down next to him and said: "Well, Tom, you're sittin' in the presence of the Wyoming Stock Grower's Association, I suppose. At least those who count.

"Most of us here are familiar with what you've done to help our industry in the past, Tom. I know you've met a few of us during the business up in Johnson County. Those who didn't know much about you and what you've accomplished have been filled in."

Coble paused for a moment and looked around the room. Most of the men were looking at him or Horn. A few looked at the floor or the oil paintings on the wall. He grimly thought that if he weren't the one doing the introducing, he'd probably be checking out a Reubens copy, too. This was no joyful business.

Across the room, Dave James removed a cigar from his mouth and exhaled a cloud a smoke. One of the earliest and most powerful cattle barons in the territory, he was known as an exceptional businessman and, sometimes, ruthless adversary. His rugged good looks belied his sixty-five years, with his thick silver hair being the only indication of his age.

"So, Tom," said James, "we've all heard you're a man to ride the trail with. I have the pleasure of knowing Miles Krone and Steve Franks who were with you under General Miles's command in Arizona. They think very highly of you."

Still holding the unlit cigar, Horn nodded and fidgeted with his hands. He smiled knowingly at the mention of his old *compañeros*.

"It's my understanding you were present at Skeleton Cañon with Lieutenant Gatewood to witness Geronimo's final surrender."

Horn began to respond to the comment as if it were a challenge, then caught himself. These men were naturally curious, and he was not one to let their thirst for knowledge go unslaked.

"Yes, sir, Mister James, I was there," he said. "Fact is, I was the interpreter for Lieutenant Gatewood, who spoke a little Spanish but no Apache, to my knowledge."

James took another puff on the cigar and said: "Tell us about Geronimo. I hear he was fearless and a master tactician."

"He was an Injun, like any other," said Horn bluntly.

An awkward silence ensued, causing Horn quickly to amend the statement. "I don't mean he was a drunken lout or nothin'. He just was pretty wore out when we finally took him in. Fact is, I think the old boy took a shine to me. He told me I was the only one he'd surrender to. Liked my name, Horn, he said."

Horn looked nervously around the room, expecting more questions about his service in Arizona. Instead, a meticulously dressed man stood from his chair and, although ostensibly talking to Horn, addressed the room.

"We'd like to thank you for coming and meeting with us, Tom," said John Stain. A man whose fortune was made early in life in Pennsylvania, Stain took to the rôle of the dandy and made no bones about enjoying his appearance as a pivotal player in frontier Wyoming. His self-image was healthy, and he thought he exuded leadership and vitality. To many, he did. But to just as many, he was merely the sycophantic underling of Governor William Ford, himself one of the most powerful and influential men in the western United States. When Ford talked, Stain listened. Whenever jokes were passed around outside of his presence, it was also mischievously insinuated that when Ford passed gas, Stain said: "Excuse me."

Stain cleared his throat and continued. "I'm sure that John Coble has done an exemplary job in explaining our position here to you, but I'd like to expand, if you will, on some of the problems we face."

Stain turned to face Horn and gave him a quizzical smile. Behind a passive face, Horn thought to himself that this could be a dangerous, ruthless man.

"As a veteran of the Johnson County fracas, you're well aware of the danger of allowing squatters and rustlers to run rampant. We have a somewhat different proposition down here. First of all, the law is generally on our side and tries to take hold of the situation and prosecute those who steal. But it's obviously a difficult situation. No one can adequately police a fifty thousand acre spread, making sure that each and every animal that belongs to us is safe.

"Now, we realize that even with a man of your reputation on board, some of these rustlers will continue to ply their trade. What we need to know from you is, if they continue, can you eventually catch them?"

Stain stopped for a moment, and took a puff on the lit cigar he was holding in his right hand. As Horn started to answer, Stain quickly interjected: "*And,* Tom, we also would like to know if you can eventually, for lack of a better term, *eradicate* them?"

Most of the men in the room seemed taken off guard by Stain's boldness, with many clearing their throats and catching each other's eyes.

Horn slowly and deliberately raised the unlit cigar he was holding to his mouth. He licked the outside, then carefully bit off the end, eschewing the silver cutter laying within reach. He pinched the cigar's end from his tongue and stuck it in his waistcoat pocket. He then reached over to the table to his right and pulled a wooden match from a small container. He flicked it against the underside of his fingernail and made a show of lighting the cigar. A ring of smoke about his head, he looked at Stain and said: "Mister Stain, *I* understand that you have problems. Now, *you* should understand that I fix those kind of problems. In this kind of business, referrals are often hard to come by, but there are those you already must have talked to, or I wouldn't be sitting here."

Horn took another puff of the cigar, then continued. "Now, here's how I look at your situation. I'm a God-fearin' and law-abidin' man, which means I understand the difference between right and wrong. When a man has property that another man takes, that's wrong. It's that simple. It's my job to get your property back and, at your discretion, punish them that took it. Sometimes the law helps, sometimes it hurts. You've got some fine lawmen here in Cheyenne, yet it's my impression that you don't want to involve them in industry matters. That's fine. I make my living because you feel that way.

"Here's how I see things. If you suspect someone of stealin' your livestock, I can go have a talk with him . . . see how he reacts. I'll guarantee you I'll know whether he's tellin' the truth or not. Once we've determined that he's done somethin' wrong, he'll either pay or we'll tell him to leave the territory. If he continues on this road to ruin, we handle things in other ways."

Once again, Horn paused to take a puff on the cigar and gauge the men's reactions. Most were staring intently at him, sucked into the conversation. They knew they were talking to the real thing now.

"And as for sheepmen, well, sheep don't belong on the range now, do they? Nasty critters, they are, only fit for Navajo and Messicans to eat. Like you, I seen fine range completely destroyed by them god-forsaken critters. Those that raise 'em have no business here. They can move to Messico if they wanna raise sheep."

The men in the room murmured their assent to Horn's opinion. He looked over at John Coble, sitting nearby, and saw the cattleman's confident smile.

The group began chatting comfortably, asking Horn questions and filling him in on the local politics and personalities involved in the livestock business. Talk turned to rustling operations, and the more well known of the cattle thieves were identified and vilified. A half hour later, Coble nodded and then stood to address the group.

"Boys, I don't think we need to go on much further. Let's get on with our business now, and I'll talk particulars with Tom here shortly."

Turning to Horn, Coble said: "Tom, I'd like to welcome you back to Wyomin' once again. If you decide you want to hook up with this outfit, I'm sure you'll be workin' with several of us in this room on a regular basis. Now, why don't you go on out and ask that hefty fella at the desk for the key to your room and a bottle of Kentucky sour mash. I'll join you directly."

Horn nodded in affirmation as he stood, grabbed his hat, and walked from the gathering, puffing on the cigar butt as he neared the door. At the exit he turned, nodded once again to the group, and quickly raised his right index finger above his right eyebrow, giving them an unexpected salute. Most of the men voiced their thanks as he left the room.

An hour later, Coble knocked on his door. When Horn let him in, he walked to the corner of the room and eyed a new maple chair with a thick, intricately embroidered seat cushion. After raising his eyebrows at the absolute luxury of the thing, he sat down and said: "We'd like you to stay, Tom. Fact is, I think you *have* to stay. This group's countin' on you already."

Settling his rear securely into the cushion, he continued: "I think you and I are gonna get along just fine, so I'll be your main man. You need anything, you come to me. Now, let's figure out what you're gonna do."

Horn and Coble spent the next two hours sipping sour mash whisky and talking about the advantages of stock detectives over deputized lawmen. They formulated a plan that would put Horn on as a cowboy at a well-known ranch, where he could spend his days investigating rustling with little scrutiny. After all, he'd merely be a cowboy on the range, searching for strays. Innocuous enough, until he found them in someone else's pasture with someone else's brand.

"What we'd like you to do," said Coble, "is join Frank Webster's spread as a hand. Now, I work with Frank, and we'll pass on the word that we've hired a pretty notable cowboy, Tom Horn.

"If that don't stop some rustlin', we'll have to take more drastic measures, but. . . ." Coble struggled momentarily with his meaning, his face somber and his eyes intense. Finally he said: "Let's just hope it don't have to come to that. Now, let's talk money. . . ."

When Coble and Horn parted that afternoon, Horn felt for the first time in ages that he had a future, that the world had not left him behind, after all. When he looked at the amber liquid in his glass, he saw many possibilities.

That was before the killings of Fred Powell and Bill Lewis. That was before killing Spaniards in Cuba. That was before the Brown's Hole business down in Colorado. That was before Willie Nickell was ambushed, his life's blood seeping into the thirsty Wyoming clay.

Horn's dreams had vanished with Willie's death, and now he sat in a stinking cell, awaiting his hanging. Only the frequent visits from John Coble, as well as those less frequent from Glendolene Kimmell, seemed to keep him sane, and now Coble spoke of bringing news.

As he and Coble began talking, the freezing wind kicked up, its mighty gusts acting as a battering ram on the side of the jailhouse. The entire structure shook, and Horn noticed snow blowing in a frenzied fury through the window. He found himself on edge, nervous. All in all, he figured it was the wind that made these people so god-damned crazy. The cattlemen, the ranchers, the rustlers, and even the sheepmen. They took offense at any slight, and pulled guns as quick as a scorpion stings an outstretched hand. It had probably rubbed off on him when he was out alone on the prairie, he decided, causing him often to ride with his hand on his rifle. Hell, even Willie Nickell knew how to use a gun, Horn reminded himself.

The constant gusts brought him an image he could not shake—an image of someone hanging from a noose looped over a branch of a lone cottonwood, his feet off the ground and his body twisting in the Wyoming wind. The people surrounding the body, looking up, held their hats on their heads to keep them from blowing away. Satisfied that the hanged man was dead, they turned and walked from the place, leaving the body to be pummeled by violent gusts, alone and helpless. He considered shaking his head violently to exorcise the image, but opted for dignity in front of his old friend.

After enough small talk to make sure one of Stephens's deputies was not listening in from the other side of the door, Coble began outlining the information he brought.

"Tom, you really done it," he began. "You stirred up a pot o' rattlers, all right." The stockman chuckled, shook his head from side to side, and continued. "Ford and Stain called for me, asked if I knew where your so-called *information* was kept. I told 'em I might be your friend, but, in this matter, I wasn't your confidant. What you could do to them would hurt me as well."

"John," Horn broke in, "you know I wouldn't. . . ."

"I know, I know," said Coble. "But they don't, and that's what's important. Anyways, Ford called a meeting. Pretty near everyone was there. Polk, Webster, James, Cooper, all of 'em. And, of course, Ford and Stain. Even Gov'ner Chatterton sent some lapdog. Stain stands up and pontificates about how we got bigger trouble'n we ever counted on. Then he reads your note, and you could damn' near hear jaws hittin' the floor all over the room. Then the sheriff steps up from the back of the room and begins talkin'.

"You know Clay Stephens is a right smart feller, Tom.

So he begins by sayin' how the populace of Cheyenne and the people of Wyomin' won't stand for another jailbreak or you slippin' away some way or t'other. They'd track you down themselves and tie you up to the nearest tree, he says. And Tom, I believe he's right. I'm sorry to say it, pard, but there's just no sympathy for you out there right now. None whatsoever."

Horn shook his head in understanding and rolled his hand in a circular motion, urging Coble to continue.

"Finally he gets to the point. Tells us that we're in for a bunch of trouble if your note gets to the U.S. Attorney in Denver. Tells 'em he's got a plan. And, it's more than passable, I must admit."

Coble smiled in wonderment as he outlined Stephens's scheme.

"You know how most executions are public? Well, it's already been decided by the powers that be, namely Ford and Stain, to make yours pretty private." Coble stopped and raised his eyebrows. "Excuse the morbidity, Tom. So Stephens says we'll work it so that this special gallows they're buildin' will be draped in keepin' with the somber occasion, and, when you fall into eternity, every one of the witnesses will swear they saw you hang. They'll see you disappear below the drape when the trap door's sprung, and they'll see the taut rope. In their minds, they'll see everything. What they won't see is you hangin' at the end of that rope. 'Cause that'll be a coupla hundred pound sacks of flour, Tom. Hell, they'll be tellin' their poker buddies about your purple face and bulgin' eyes for the rest of their days, and not one of 'em will actually see you hang. It's a magician's trick, Tom."

Coble stared at Horn's disbelieving expression. Almost giggling, he reached over and grabbed Horn's upper arm.

"Tom," he said, "they're gonna sprint you outta there and give you more money than you could ever use . . . long as you spend it in Mexico."

Taken aback, Horn was speechless for a moment. Then it all came into focus. It was a beautiful plan. Let everybody think he was strung up. Then somehow, with a slipknot or something, have him shake loose. No more Tom Horn to deal with. They'd think he was moldering away six feet under, food for the worms. They'd tell stories about how little Willie's killer met his fate on a frigid, windy day in Cheyenne. Meantime, he'd be sippin' mescal and *aguardiente* in Nogales or Juárez under another name.

He realized he was being given a new chance. The image of a wind-tossed body hanging alone on the prairie subsided as he realized that he'd gambled with the skill of his father, and he'd won.

"Details," Tom Horn said. "Gimme details."

Chapter Six

He was an Injun, like any other.

Horn laughed out loud when he thought of his response to Dave James's comment at that first meeting long ago. Now, sitting on his cot with his back to the rough brick wall, reflecting on his life in a dank Cheyenne jail cell following John Coble's departure, he felt deep in his core that he would give anything he ever owned to see the old warrior once again. In fact, if he got out of this scrape alive, he'd maybe try to hustle on down to Fort Sill and visit the old boy.

Horn thought how Geronimo had a great sense of humor and loved a good joke. He'd fancy telling him about the mischief that would soon be going on in Cheyenne—how the whole world would see Tom Horn hanged and sent off to his grave with no never mind, only to have him show up punchin' cattle and whores in Chihuahua. *Yep,* he thought, *them Apaches'd think this 'un's a stitch, all right.*

He didn't understand why he had answered James in such a frivolous manner at that fateful meeting. It had made him feel guilty afterward. He had rationalized at the time that James had no business knowing anything about the great Chiricahua war chief. He had done it out of respect for Geronimo, he decided, although a corner of what had once been his conscience told him he lied just to be contrary.

To him, Geronimo was anything but just another Indian. He was, along with Al Sieber and Edward Plummer, one of the handful of men Horn had ever come to respect. He smiled and let loose a small chuckle when he thought back to those early years, how he'd met and matched up with those giants of the frontier.

When Horn lit out from Missouri on his father's gelding, he knew only that he was headed into a great adventure and told himself to be ready for it. It didn't take long in coming.

Even a superior shot like Horn gets hungry riding across the forever prairie, and, after five days, he found he was hungry, indeed. The windswept terrain was nearly devoid of trees, and the only sign of people he ran across was a double set of wagon tracks that seemed to lead alternately south, then southwest. Following the tracks, he found himself cresting a ridge, only to see a small town situated on a broad plain above a stream a couple of miles to the south. He wondered why the place was in such a desolate location until he heard the distant bellow of a train's whistle and saw the black smoke in the distance, off to the east. Like a hundred other towns, this one had been constructed on the prairie to serve the railroad.

Riding into the tiny town, he discovered he was in Newton, Kansas. He dismounted in front of a watering trough and let the tired gelding drink its fill. He then led the horse past the newly built hotel, the meat market, and the creamery, stopping before the railroad agent's office before tying its reins to the hitching post. The train he had seen had come and gone, and the station showed no signs of life save for the flickering of a gas lamp that could be seen through a small, dingy window. Pounding his hat against his leg to get the dust off, he stepped across the boardwalk and entered the tiny brick building.

Burlington Northern agent Thad Stanton looked up from copying a set of train orders and nodded at Horn. A man of about forty-five, with a ring of gray hair around his bald pate, he wore a rumpled light gray flannel suit. He held his finger up, indicating a small wait was in order. Tom stood with his hat in his hand in the stifling room, feeling sweat run between his shoulder blades and waiting patiently while letting his eyes adjust to the dark surroundings. He looked around the room and saw only the mahogany desk and chair used by the agent, as well as a small telegraph machine that clattered now and again.

When Stanton finished, he blew on the flimsy paper to dry the ink, looked up, and pleasantly said: "Well, now. What can I do for you, son?"

Tom cleared his throat and said: "I need work, sir."

Stanton chuckled and said in his surprisingly high voice: "Well, don't we all, son? Don't we all? I don't know that there's work to be done."

He looked the young man over, noted his trail-worn appearance, and asked: "You live around here, son? I don't believe I've seen you."

"No, sir," Horn answered. "I'm headed west from Missouri. Plan on goin' to Denver City or maybe even on to California. I . . . ," he paused, wanting to say more but worried that word of his father's beating might have been sent over the telegraph. "I need work, that's all."

"Well, provided the Indians don't fill you full of arrows and you don't starve to death, the West is indeed a place of opportunity for a young man such as yourself. I met the great man Mister Greeley once myself, you know, at about the time he issued his call for the nation's youth to forge on westward. He was at an Opera House in Saint Joe and talked about visitin' Denver City and pullin' gold out of the rivers when it was nothin' but tents and latrines. Oh," he chuckled, "there I go again, carryin' on."

Stanton stood, stretched, and said: "I swear, sitting in this chair all day and half the night is as trying as ridin' with Bloody Bill." He raised his eyebrows and gave Horn a little grin. "Figure of speech, you know," he explained. "You have any special skills, son?"

Tom eagerly answered: "Well, sir, I can shoot the eye out of a varmint at a hundred and fifty yards or more, and I can ride 'most good as anybody."

"Fine credentials, indeed, if we needed a hunter to provide meat. But those days are gone, son, long gone. So's the meat, by the way." He chuckled. Stanton sat back down and cracked his knuckles. He said: "What's your name?"

"Tom Horn."

"Well, Tom Horn, the only work I have is temporary, at best, which probably suits your plans, seeing as how you're headed west and all. We're layin' track out to the west a couple of miles, eventually build a roundhouse, I suppose. It takes a strong back and a weak mind, as they say, but it's work. Seein' as you're a good-size boy, I don't think you'd have much trouble workin' the rails."

Stanton saw the eagerness in Horn's eyes. "Dollar a day wages," he said. "Should be done in about two or three weeks. Suit your fancy?"

Horn nodded and smiled.

Stanton reached into his desk, took out a gray piece of paper, and scribbled a quick note with an old style quill pen. Handing it to Horn, he said: "Ride due west until you see a crew working. Give this to the foreman, Dan Roule. He'll set you up. You can camp out there or stay here in town at the hotel, it makes no never mind."

The agent reached once more into the desk and flipped a

silver dollar toward Horn. "Here's an advance on your first day's wages, Horn. You look hungry. Get yourself on over to the hotel and eat as much as you can hold." He turned back to his train orders and said: "It's hard work out there."

Horn thanked the agent and left the office, on his way to the hotel's restaurant. Years later, he would remember Stanton with great charity and often wondered whatever became of the man who so casually had led him down his life's path.

Three weeks later, he rode west once again, his muscles toned by fourteen-hour days of setting rails, and sixteen of the twenty-one dollars he'd earned stashed in his saddlebag. He'd worked side-by-side with a huge Irishman named Flynn who had been to the West and was working his way back toward Philadelphia after going bust in Colorado's gold fields. Flynn regaled Horn with stories of the Rockies, and particularly of the high desert and beautiful mountains of New Mexico and Colorado. From Flynn, Horn learned the approximate co-ordinates of the Santa Fé Trail, and decided that New Mexico Territory was for him.

Now he rode up the long alluvial grade formed by the Río Grande, and stopped on a hill overlooking the old city of Santa Fé. He was astonished.

Santa Fé in 1875 was more than seventeen-year-old Horn could have imagined. A western crossroads for nearly three hundred years, it seamlessly melded Anglo, Spanish, and Indian cultures in a heady mixture of commerce, spirituality, and outright danger. Founded as a Spanish outpost in New Spain, Santa Fé in the 19th Century existed to make money. It was the hub of the westward expansion and the supply line to California. Buckskin-clad hunters and scouts walked the hard-packed streets and plazas next to fancily dressed businessmen. Mexican *vaqueros* rode side-by-side with cowboys while gentlemen gamblers and vicious murderers alike staked their lives at the gaming tables. Priests tended their beautifully ornate churches. Santa Fé was bursting at the seams. It was absolutely *alive*.

For young Tom Horn, Santa Fé was a cradle of opportunity. Unlike the prairie towns of the Great Plains, Santa Fé offered a wide variety of employment for those with Horn's abilities as a hunter and horseman. Nestled in the rolling Sangre de Cristo Mountains, the town was still truly on the frontier and, as such, desperately needed those who knew their way around firearms. It also needed men who could handle horses. Horn thought he had found paradise on earth.

A few days after hitting town, Horn walked into the adobe office of the Overland Stage Company and asked for work. In an effort to look presentable, he had spent one of his remaining four dollars on a room and two more on two new denim shirts and a pair of sturdy broadcloth trousers. He then bathed in the Santa Fé River, being careful to choose a site upstream in order to avoid the town's sewage. Knowing that the stage company employed those who could shoot well, he carried the Winchester he had stolen from his father in its long, fitted leather boot.

Upon hearing the young man in the doorway in stiff new clothes inquire about work, the company's agent, Samuel Charon, quietly stood and motioned for Horn to follow. They walked back out the door and around the rear of the building, then followed a path down to the river, Charon expectorating from a plug of tobacco all the way. When they stopped, Charon pointed to a rock outcropping nearly two hundred yards distant.

"See that white rock on the overhang above the river?" he asked.

Horn squinted and mumbled in the affirmative.

"Shoot it," said Charon, while stepping away a few paces.

Horn quickly unsheathed the rifle, pumped a round into the chamber, and smoothly raised the gun to his shoulder. Barely aiming, he squeezed the trigger, felt the shock of the rifle, and watched the rock shatter into sand.

Charon spit on the sandy loam of the riverbank, said— "Young eyes, awright."—and motioned for Horn to follow him back to the office. On the way, he said: "How are you with hosses?"

"Just about perfect," Horn boasted.

Inside the office, Charon sat in a low-backed oak chair, opened a ledger, and said: "You start tomorrow. You'll be working with Hans Breiten, driving the Overland stage 'tween here 'n' Prescott."

"Prescott?" queried Horn, unaware of any town with the name.

"Yeah," answered Charon, looking at Horn quizzically. "Over to Arizona Territory." He shook his head in mock disgust and said: "Now, what's yer name, boy?"

Twenty-five dollars a month seemed like all the sultan's gold to Tom Horn, who took to the life of a Western man like a duck to water. Hans Breiten was a huge, ham-fisted man who knew the country like few others, and took it upon himself to teach Horn the ropes. It was a matter of self-preservation, he figured. There was no use being surly to somebody who might be called upon to save your life.

Catching Horn squinting into the sun on their first run, he transferred the reins to one hand and, shaking his fist at the sky, said: "Never stare at the sun, boy. Never stare at the fire. *Never*. A blind look-out is more useless than a one-armed carpenter."

Horn looked at Breiten, gave him a peeved look, and, out of sheer contrariness, continued to check out the bright sky. Breiten just shoved a plug of tobacco into his mouth and began to spit off the side of the stage.

A few miles farther on, Breiten slowed the stage and pointed toward a distant promontory. "See that Injun?" he said.

Horn looked to where Breiten was pointing and strained to see anything. He started to think Breiten was playing a trick, until his eyes adjusted and he saw a lone figure outlined against the sky. He started to raise his rifle, but was stopped by the beefy Dutchman.

"Naw!" he yelled. "If he let us see him, he ain't posin' us no threat. We must have nothin' they want today. Now, git the sun outta yer eyes afore we both die from yer neglect."

Chastened, Horn resolved never to let such a situation arise again. Of course, many did. Yet, each time, he listened to Breiten's common sense and stored it away, slowly adopting his huge partner's combination of wisdom and caution.

Horn learned each of Breiten's little lessons well, and was saddened when Charon called him in a few months later with a new assignment.

"We need somebody to move and guard stock. Apaches've been stealing us blind. I want you to move some hosses 'n' mules on down to Camp Verde for the Army. Stay down there and herd 'em for a while. You might want to pick up a little of the Messican tongue from some-uh the *vaqueros* you'll meet. Comes in handy around here, *Señor* Horn."

The Verde River cut into land claimed by the Apaches, and Horn was quick to understand the animosities that existed between Anglos, Mexicans, and Indians. He and two others managed to deliver the animals, but watched over the next months as many were either stolen or maimed by the Apaches in an effort to slow down the Army's encroachment.

During his time on the Verde, Horn managed to adapt well to a cowboy's life, a *vaquero*'s life actually. His companions all spoke Spanish, and he discovered he possessed an innate ability to decipher and understand languages other than English. At length, his horsemanship and his command of "Messican" caused him to be retained by the Army and put in charge of the quartermaster's herd in Prescott, at Fort Whipple.

On a breathlessly hot July day, while moving several horses out of the rotation, Horn wiped the back of his hand across his eyes to clear the sweat, and found himself looking at what he first thought was a specter. Seated on a fence only ten feet away, the figure seemed to have appeared from nowhere. He was dressed in lightly tanned, faded, and worn buckskin leggings with an unbleached cotton shirt and moccasins that seemed to fit him like skin. The man relaxed easily on the top tier of the corral. He appeared gaunt and lean, but wiry. His clean-shaven face was brown as a berry from the Arizona sun, and his battered old hat shaded his eyes, making it hard for Horn to ascertain his age.

After staring at Horn for a few moments, the man jumped from the corral and walked forward, gently grabbing the gelding's bridle and nuzzling the horse. He looked up and said in a gravelly voice: "Heard ye're the one speaks Messican. That straight?"

Horn nodded his assent.

"Speak it pretty good, do ya?"

"Good enough," said Horn.

Then the conversation continued in Spanish. "Good enough for an old horse like me to understand?"

"Yes, well enough for even the mules in the herd."

The man cracked a small smile and said: "Haven't been called a mule in an age, but I suppose I asked for it."

He reached his hand up to Horn and said: "Name's Al Sieber. I'm looking for an interpreter."

Horn's eyes widened, and he took the hand and shook it. Sieber was a respected scout and Indian fighter, and as Chief of Scouts for the 5th Cavalry was now busy ensuring the peace as well as chasing renegade Apaches all over hell and back. Horn had heard his name spoken in reverential tones ever since he had passed into the Southwest.

"Tom Horn," the startled rider said, introducing himself.

Sieber continued to hold the horse's bridle while he talked to Horn, switching back to English. "I heerd from the adjutant you picked up Messican quick and easy like, and I need a good spirit to work with me down to the San Carlos Agency, help us talk to those Apaches what speak Messican. Said you knew hossflesh, too."

"Yep, I do," said Horn.

"Well . . . ?" said Sieber, letting the question hang.

In Horn's mind, there was no choice but to go with Sieber. When a man looking for adventure finds adventure, there's no stopping him.

"When do we leave?" he asked, and watched Sieber raise his eyebrows in acknowledgement.

"Somethin' you oughta know," said Sieber. "Last feller called me a mule died in memorable fashion."

As Sieber walked away, Horn thought the scout's raucous laughter would spook the entire herd.

Chapter Seven

The following years rivaled and even surpassed Horn's boyhood dreams of adventure with the James Gang. Al Sieber was the genuine article, one of the true frontiersmen whose lineage began with Lew Wetzel and Daniel Boone and carried on through Jim Bridger, Kit Carson, and Tom Tobin. While serving under Sieber's command, Horn combined his natural instincts with a thousand intangibles imparted by the great scout. He learned the art of silent tracking, becoming able to follow an enemy through the roughest terrain with little overt sign. Often, intuition was as important as any physical evidence left by those being tracked, and he quickly picked up Sieber's ability to judge the probable actions and reactions of those he followed.

"There's one thing you must always tell yerself," Sieber said at least a thousand times. "The Apache is the finest fighter in the world. There's none better. He's better'n you. He's better'n me. We just have to fight smarter an' hope there's more of us."

Sieber and Horn were on a scouting mission in the spring of 1882, quietly searching for a small band of renegades led by Florio, a firebrand who had visions of the destruction of all whites. The command sent the two south, toward San Bernardino Springs, on a reconnaissance mission. They had dismounted and walked their horses for some miles, tying them to a scrub oak when they ascertained the proximity of an Indian camp. They continued on foot, carefully picking their way through the rough cholla and underbrush. As Horn made his way upwind toward the faint smell of campfire smoke, he suddenly sensed someone in a parallel course off to his right. He drew his gun and turned quickly, hoping to get whoever it was in his sights. Nothing.

His heart was beating hard, and he was nauseous with fear. Pulling himself under as much control as he could muster, he continued forward another hundred yards until he heard the quick snapping of fingers that was Sieber's sign for danger. He ensconced himself in a hollow and remained absolutely motionless. Within minutes, he heard brush rattle off to his left, and then behind him. He remained motionless, waiting for some signal from Sieber.

Listening intently, he heard a single shot to the east. Immediately two Apache warriors glided through the brush within twenty yards, silently moving in the direction of the shot. Just as quickly and quietly, he rose and followed the two Indians. Ahead, he saw them stop and raise their rifles. Without thinking, he immediately brought his Winchester repeater up and shot, hitting the warrior on the left in the back, causing him to leap forward with a great gasp, dying before he hit the ground. Horn instantly turned the rifle on the remaining Apache, firing and hitting him underneath the arm as he turned. He saw the impact as the bullet hit its target and saw the hatred in the man's face as he went down.

Unconsciously Horn hit the dirt and rolled to the right, just as two bullets hit the spot where he had been standing. Two more shots came out of nowhere, and he heard choked cries. Then, seconds later, the sound of Sieber's snapping fingers crackled through the crisp air, followed by his low voice.

"I think we got 'em, Tom. At least four of 'em. Let's backtrack, hoss."

Trying to will the rush of blood to his temples from sounding like a locomotive, Horn retreated as quickly as possible. Within a half hour, he reached the horses, only to find Sieber mounted and ready to ride.

"What took ya, hoss?" he said, looking toward their back trail.

Horn sat on an uprooted willow and tried to stop shaking. With a great sigh, he looked at Sieber and said: "What happened back there?"

"I told ya them Apache's is like spirits, and they are," Sieber answered. "I thought we could get to they camp afore they found us, but we didn't. One of 'em, prob'ly Florio, snuck up to my right. I had to shoot him, which was prob'ly a lucky thing fer you. When I shot, them two came runnin' toward me, and I saw 'em go down by your hand. I believe ye kilt one. The other 'n' I don't know about.

"Then another 'n' pops up and commences to shoot at you. I got him . . . the one they call Joaquín at the agency."

Horn put his head in his hands momentarily, then stood. "Now what?" he said.

"Now, we get back to San Carlos," said Sieber. "The Apache women have already retrieved their bodies. They'll give 'em proper rites. We have to go back and make our report . . ."—he laughed grimly—"put the fear of God into those Injuns that want to buck the Great Father."

Horn spent weeks trying to rectify what had happened in his mind. He had wounded and perhaps killed two men who were trying to kill him. But why? Was there a way it could have been prevented? He didn't know. There were times he felt as if he could have killed his father, but then by most folks' reckoning, his father deserved it. He hadn't even known these men. Hadn't even known their true names, just the Spanish names they had acquired.

He had seen what Apaches did to their captives, the unspeakable agony and mutilation they put their enemies through. He tried to scorn them for it. Yet he still realized their hatred was righteous. In the end, he decided that thinking too much about it would only get him killed. He determined to carry on.

He spent much time with the Apache scouts, tribal members who worked for the Army, helping to track and capture the renegades among their own people as well as those of other tribes. It was from these men that he began to understand the lives and customs of the Apaches, and to empathize with their plight.

At the San Carlos Agency, Horn's proclivity for languages surfaced once again. Rather than translating the Apache's Spanish into English, he reasoned it would be much easier to translate directly from the source. Within months, he had learned enough Apache to communicate, and within a year was as fluent as a white man could be.

By 1883, Horn had met and spoken with most of the influential Chiricahua warriors, translating their concerns to the Army brass. Since General George Crook had left, there was absolutely no trust in the government on the part of the Apaches. Crook's word was law, and the Apache people respected the fact that he never lied to them. After his reassignment, reservation conditions went from abysmal to horrific, and several of the leaders, including the surly yet brilliant Geronimo, had left the agency, occupying the mountains to the south. They conducted savage raids on both white and Mexican settlers, sparing no one, man, woman, or child. These same leaders trusted few whites, but Horn was among those they at least did not disdain.

Sieber had spread word of the fight at San Bernardino Springs, and that Horn had fought and vanquished his enemies with great skill and dignity. He was a warrior, to be respected.

Gradually he became the primary conduit of communication between Anglos and Indians; a man who could not only translate words, but meaning as well. His understanding of the language was such that the great war chief Juh bestowed him with the name Talking Boy.

The first time Horn met Geronimo face to face was when the peerless warrior joined others in the Apache hierarchy to meet with the San Carlos agent to document the latest round of broken promises made by Washington. Uneasiness hung in the air like visible haze for days before the morning of the gathering. Agent, traders, and soldiers alike were uneasy, knowing that each side had absolutely no reservations about butchering the other.

Horn was amazed by the gathering that took place in the agent's quarters. The Apaches had arrived in near silence, as usual, their small ponies seeming to glide in from the morning mirages on the desert's horizon. Others arrived on foot, equally unobtrusive.

Seven Apache leaders including Juh and Geronimo entered and stood before the agent's desk. The agent remained sitting, disdainful of the delegation. The man was crooked as a mountain road, and was diverting a good portion of the funds appropriated for the Indians' welfare into a safe under the floorboards in his quarters, and from there into a private account in a St. Louis bank. The agent's job was a gold mine, and he wasn't about to do anything to change it.

After a tense silence, Horn rose and, with wide eyes aimed toward the floor and a wildly pumping heart, told

Juh that he would turn their words into English to be understood by the agent. He could feel Geronimo's flat black eyes on him, but kept his own eyes downcast in deference to Juh. Geronimo favored Juh with a look and said: "This is Talking Boy. You say he will make our thoughts and words enter the head of the agent?"

Juh nodded affirmatively as Horn raised his eyes to acknowledge Geronimo's comments.

Geronimo nodded gravely, then looked toward the agent and said: "Good, because the agent's head has nothing in it now."

Several of the Apache delegation looked disapprovingly at Geronimo, but Horn could not help smiling at the joke, letting out a soft snort as he stared at the floor. The suspicious agent immediately asked what was said, and Horn lied: "He said that Talking Boy is a man, and that I should turn their words into the language of the Great Father."

The meeting was a disaster for the Apaches. The agent spoke to them arrogantly, as if they were children, and Horn was obliged to translate accurately. When it was apparent that no reconciliation of their grievances would be achieved, the seven men abruptly left in somber moods. Horn followed them outside, where he watched Geronimo break from the others and walk toward the corrals used by Indians for their horses. For a brief moment, he turned and locked eyes with Horn, then was gone.

Shortly after, most of the Apache leaders removed their people to the southern mountains, becoming renegades and, in the process, murdering any whites they came across. Theirs was a holy war, but their gods had deserted them. Their fate was sealed. By late 1883, General Crook was reassigned to the 5th Cavalry, and set out to bring in the renegades and restore order. In his gruff manner, he publicly humiliated and dismissed the corrupt agent and set out to restore dignity to the Apaches. Sieber and Horn were often on the point, scouting out the Apache camps and strongholds throughout the blistering desert and advising Crook and his officers about strategy.

The summer of 1885 was crucial to Crook's attempt to quell the Apache uprising. Many of the Chiricahua Apache war chiefs had taken advantage of amnesty, bringing their people to the San Carlos agency at Crook's behest. They were tired and starving, and knew their debilitating, costly war was over.

Geronimo, however, stayed in the field and continued his raids on Mexican and American settlements. His bravery in battle was legendary, but his savagery was distancing even those, both Indian and white, who felt kinship with his cause.

That July, Sieber and Horn were charged to meet and brief the newly assigned adjutant of the 5th Regimental Battalion, Edward Plummer. A graduate of the U.S. Military Academy's first class, Plummer had served on the Texas frontier and for the last year had been stationed at Fort Union, New Mexico. Horn expected the column approaching the San Carlos Agency to be commanded by a stiff military man, a know-nothing academician capable only of understanding European battle strategies. Plummer defied his preconceptions immediately.

After reporting to Crook and his officers, Plummer met Sieber and Horn on their own ground, at the regimental corral. He walked across the dusty commons, squinting into the bright sunlight and made directly for the scouts. A man of medium height and erect bearing, he greeted the frontiersmen cautiously, yet cordially. Wearing the broad-brimmed military hat favored on the frontier, he nonetheless had the look of someone completely at ease in what must have been an incredibly foreign place. His blue eyes were piercing, but somehow nonjudgmental. Even to Sieber, who held few men in esteem, it was obvious that Plummer was a leader.

After exchanging what passed for pleasantries on the frontier, Plummer turned a full circle, looking at every aspect of the never-ending horizon. When he stopped, he was once again facing the scouts. Still looking up, he said in his clipped Yankee accent: "Remember where you came from, gentlemen? Remember living among people, where there were trees and buildings and clouds, always clouds? The sky was never this big. Even on the ocean, it never seemed this immense."

The scouts inadvertently looked upward into the clear blue, Plummer's musing leaving them wondering if they had, indeed, forgotten their past lives. Looking at the incredible expanse of sky told them why they had left, why they had come West, and why they would never leave. Plummer's voice broke the spell.

"I have no doubt that you think me a stupid Easterner, the same type of arrogant jackass as most of my predecessors," he said, his eyes twinkling. "I'll do all I can to dispel that impression."

Sieber and Horn looked at each other and broke out laughing. Sieber immediately offered the new officer a plug of tobacco, which was declined, and said: "So, what're our orders?"

Plummer fixed a stare on the scout and said: "Your first order, sir, is to tell me everything you know. Take days or weeks if you must, but teach me about the Apaches. Take me into the mind of Geronimo."

Horn was dumbfounded. The majority of officers he had

observed, particularly those whose commands came after the Civil War, were rigid, always attempting to fit situations into their own preconceived notions. Now, here was someone actually attempting to understand the circumstances connected with subduing the Apaches.

The three men began immediately. For the next two weeks, they were inseparable, save for Plummer's official duties. Always probing, always adapting his logic to fit the conditions, Plummer little by little absorbed the nuances of Apache culture. He met at length with the agency's Apache scouts, and rode with them on several scouting forays, attempting to learn any scrap of information that might be relevant to the situation.

One evening after mess, Plummer walked through the twilight toward the barracks, accompanied as always by Sieber and Horn. The blood red sunset contrasted with the deep azure sky that deepened to black on the eastern horizon, and a few stars were beginning to show through. Plummer's incessant questioning was by now expected, and the scouts often found themselves unsure of answers.

As they walked, Plummer was uncharacteristically quiet, puffing on a cigar. For the first time, Horn felt uneasy around him. Before reaching the barracks, Plummer abruptly stopped and addressed Sieber.

"Does Geronimo realize he can't win?"

It was a question that had not been asked over the past weeks, and it startled Horn and Sieber. They, of course, never gave a second thought to the outcome of the conflict between the bureaucracy and the Apache, so they never had to challenge their certainty. The outcome was simple. There were more whites with more guns, better guns. Of course, Geronimo would lose. Yet, they never asked themselves the question that got to the heart of the matter. Did

Geronimo *know* he would lose?

Sieber started to answer and then let out a sigh. He took a dip of tobacco from an oilskin pouch he was carrying and stuffed it into his cheek. He pushed it around with his tongue until it was satisfactorily ensconced, and then spoke. "Yeah, I reckon he knows he cain't win. But he ain't no dreamer, if that's yer meanin'. We ain't facin' Cheyenne medicine men 'n' dog soldiers 'n' sech. Them Apaches, they're as practical 'n' hard-headed as any old mule."

He spat an amber glob on the dusty ground and continued. "Apaches've been runnin' since they can remember. Always bein' fought and beat by somebody. Afore white folks came, and, even after, they lived up north on the great wide plains. They warred with their neighbors, like all Injuns. Prob'ly didn't come out on the top end o' things too often, neither. The Sioux drove 'em out of the high plains, I hear. Then the Comanches latched onto hosses somehow and drove the Apaches south, here into the cholla and sand. Legend says most Apaches were killed by the Comanches. You ever see a Comanche ride a hoss, an' you'll believe it. More bowlegged than a Texas whore and a terror to behold. The best hossmen I ever seen.

"When the Apaches got here, there was nobody wanted this chunk-uh burnin' hell, so they took it. They took to the sand and wind and scorpions and cactus like perfume to a rose. They made it theirs. But they was smart. They realized they was beat and drove out afore, and that somebody's likely to try again. So they took the land and worked with it. They became the finest secret fighters in the world.

"You know what a secret fighter does, don't ya, Lieutenant? He fights with his wits. Cheyenne or Crow'll come at you with all of his proud plumage showin', just beggin' ya to shoot him down. Not the Apache. No, sir. He'll hide, go without food and water for days, actually make hisself part of the land, just to kill an enemy. Now, it's not a lack of pride, this secret fightin' business. It's not like the white man, who's proud-uh standin' in the open and takin' on all comers. It's more a common sense sorta thing. Sneakin' around may be cowardly to us. To them, it's smart.

"Don't know as I disagree with 'em," he said, chuckling. "Like I said, Apaches been moved around and drove out of near 'bout everywhere. This is all they got left." He paused shortly, raised a finger, and wagged it gently at Plummer's chest. Gravely he said: "They'll do anythin' to keep it."

Sieber spit once again into the dust. "Does Geronimo know he's done fer? Hell, yes. But he's not about to give some sweet-smellin' Indian agent the satisfaction of sayin' they brought the great Geronimo to his knees. Hell, no. He's gonna run and fight till they's no fight left."

Horn was lost in his own reverie, seeing the implacable face of Geronimo in the agent's office, and fitting it to Sieber's description. He agreed, of course, that Geronimo knew it was only a matter of time before all was lost. But he didn't think the warrior thought he and his people were doomed. One look at the man's face told you that.

Plummer nodded at Sieber's information and stood looking up into the sky, his face a mask of concentration. He looked at the two men and said: "I'm sure you're right, Al. He's obviously not stupid. But I think you may be wrong about something. I suspect he *is* a dreamer. How could you not be and still lead your people? Still command them to undergo these hardships?"

He paused for a short moment, and, speaking deliberately, he said: "Well, the fact is that General Crook wants us to attempt a meeting . . . a meeting where terms are dealt and assurances are given. I'll make my report, and officers will be chosen for the detail. You gentlemen, of course, will work with the Apache scouts in an effort to locate Geronimo. Since he's likely in Mexico, we could be in for a difficult affair."

"Difficult affair's right, Lieutenant," said Sieber. "Iffen the Apaches don't skin us alive, the Messicans'll blow our heads off."

Horn broke in. "You're right, Al, but I s'pose we gotta try. I can't imagine traipsin' all over this country for the rest of my life, always chasin' Apaches that can't be caught."

"Absolutely right, Tom," said Plummer. "We have to bring him in now, for his sake and ours."

The next morning, Sieber took off before dawn with two Apache scouts, Ernesto and Pioka. Horn stayed behind with Plummer in order to interpret the seemingly endless meetings between Army officers and already-surrendered Apaches. For the next few days, his head swam with fast and furious dialogue, as plans were made and bargains were struck. It was at that time he truly earned the name Talking Boy.

Nearly three weeks after they had left the agency, Sieber and the two scouts reappeared, haggard and covered with trail dust. Sieber merely waved at Horn as he rode his run-down horse directly to the officers' quarters to give his report. Later, Horn found him in a deep sleep in the barracks. His curiosity had to wait until the next morning, when Sieber woke him and the two walked to the mess.

"Word was sent, Tom. We found several of Geronimo's boys down south o' the springs. Ernesto told 'em what we was up to, tryin' to set up a big powwow and such. They took off, and three days later I'm pullin' water outta the creek when the old boy shows up hisself."

"Geronimo?" asked Horn, amazed.

"Hell, yes. I never been snuck up on like that afore. Had no idea he was around. Could 'a' kilt me where I stood. Instead, he walks up the trail to the camp and sits crosslegged afore the fire. Talks with Ernesto fer a while, points at me, then disappears into the brush. He agreed to meet. He wants Crook hisself to show up, but the old general won't do no such thing. He's sendin' Britton Davis out to palaver. Wants Plummer 'n' me to go along."

Horn assessed the situation, and decided he felt overlooked. Having been around Sieber for some time and understanding the man's bluntness, he would never show it. But he felt slighted, nonetheless.

As they entered the mess, Sieber looked at Horn with an almost nonexistent smile and said: "He wants you to be there, too."

Surprised, Horn said: "General Crook mentioned me?"

"No, no. *Geronimo*'s askin' fer ye. Said he wants Talkin' Boy there to put his ideas into Crook's head."

The rest was a blur. Preparations began immediately. The danger and political intrigue of the ride south across the border was lost in the excitement of the upcoming meeting. Lieutenant Davis kept Horn, Plummer, and Sieber with him continuously.

The meeting itself seemed anticlimactic to Horn, even though the group faced the double danger of meeting with hostile Apaches on Mexican land. Davis met with Geronimo in a clearing at the base of two sloping foothills. A small creek bubbled through the clearing, banked by stunted willows and underbrush. A single oak grew near a shaded hillock, and the two groups met in its shade.

Geronimo seemed insulted that Crook himself hadn't come, but then his sentries who had silently reconnoitered the Army outfit for days had already told him the general was nowhere to be found. Davis presented the hard line that Crook would meet only at San Carlos, nowhere else.

It was Plummer who suggested the ultimate strategy to Crook and Davis days before. Although this might seem a poker game, Geronimo held no aces. The Mexican army was after him for raids on Mexican villages. The U.S. Army was doing the same. Yet, surrender meant dishonor. Geronimo could only surrender, said Plummer, under the assurance of amnesty and the restoration of some part of Apache land. Because the Apache people trusted Crook and only Crook, his word would be binding.

Facing Geronimo, Davis said: "If you and your warriors and your families leave Mexico now and move north to meet with the Army at San Carlos, the Great Father will not seek revenge on you for the war you have waged these past years."

The Apache chief's face showed no emotion as Horn translated Britton's conditions, yet he spoke uncharacteristically quickly. Turning to Horn, he said: "Talking Boy, is this true, or is it lies . . . more words of deceit?"

Horn thought for a moment, wanting to make sure to answer with absolute certainty. He then said: "The words I tell you are what is spoken."

"But are they true?"

Geronimo's eyes bored into Horn's, seeming to fill his soul. Knowing he was likely lying, but unable to do anything about it, Horn swallowed hard and answered. "Yes, they are true."

An hour later, negotiations were done, and Geronimo, the great war chief of the Apaches, had promised to bring his people back under the subjugation of the United States Army.

America's Indian wars were, in essence, finished.

Geronimo had one more fling at fighting the Army, engaging in one more battle and subsequently offering to surrender to Lieutenant Emmett Crawford. But he didn't show up for a few more months, which Horn attributed to his contrary sense of irony as much as his pride.

In the meantime, people and circumstances changed drastically. Crawford was killed and Horn wounded in a battle with Mexican troops while reconnoitering the renegade Apaches. Crook had enough of pounding his head against the bureaucracy. He requested and was granted reassignment. Luckily his replacement, General Nelson Miles, was a man cut from the same cloth, although he was equally unsuccessful in getting Washington realistically to address the Apache situation.

Edward Plummer was reassigned to Datil Creek, New Mexico, and from there was assigned as the acting agent of the Navajo and Moqui Indian tribes.

Sieber took off for God knows where, and Horn was named Chief of Scouts.

With those he served beside gone, Horn felt a distinct loneliness at Skeleton Cañon in September of 1886 when Geronimo surrendered for the final time to Lieutenant Gatewood. But he had no time for pining when the warrior made it clear he would speak through no one save Talking Boy.

Following the negotiations that resulted in the absolute surrender of the Chiricahua Apaches, Gatewood and Horn prepared to lead the renegades back to the San Carlos agency. As they readied to leave, Geronimo solemnly addressed Horn. "Talking Boy, I remember a time when I insulted a deceitful agent at San Carlos. You smiled while others, Apache warriors all, quaked like women."

It dawned on Horn that he was being complimented. He smiled again, as he had all that time ago, and the two nodded to each other. When Gatewood asked him what had been said, Horn repeated the old lie. "He said that Talking Boy is a man, and that I should turn his words into the language of the Great Father."

Now, seventeen years later, Horn sat in a Cheyenne jail cell and couldn't help but smile at the memories. He remembered getting sideways with General Miles. He could still hear the old boy loudly relieving him of command, then sheepishly reinstating him when it turned out that he was the only white man Geronimo would speak to.

He remembered visiting Edward Plummer in New Mexico, before he went on to Fort Sill as agent in charge of Geronimo and his disenfranchised band. Before long he became Captain Plummer, and Horn followed him to Cuba. He could still feel the strong handshake, the clap on the shoulder, and the genuine friendship of the man.

He remembered the days with Sieber, learning the ways of the land, learning to drink strong whisky and mescal, and learning that, after all is said and done, life is cheap.

He remembered the agony caused by the Mexican bullet, and taking control of his contingent after Lieutenant Crawford went down. He remembered the Mexican dead and the feeling, equal parts triumph, relief, and hollowness, that followed.

He missed those times so badly he ached. They were before he had become cavalier about life—living it and taking it. He knew when he left Arizona and headed north that the old ways were gone, yet he refused to believe it. He told himself the Wild West would go on forever, that his rough and tumble life did not have to go the way of the buffalo, the way of Geronimo and Crawford and Sieber.

That was before he had found himself drunk in Denver with a telegram from John Coble in his hand. Before he started drinking to relive the excitement of the old times. Before he took to riding around the war zone in Cuba like a damned lunatic. Before he had responded to the coy flirtations of a schoolmarm infatuated with the reputation of a gunman. Before he started hiding behind boulders to shoot people who stole cattle. Before the death of Willie Nickell.

Standing up from the sagging cot, he stretched his arms high into the air until his back cracked and his long-tailed shirt pulled up and away from the waistband of his trousers. He watched the thin shadow of his head and shoulders on the opposite wall mimic his actions and looked back into the light coming through the obscured, barred window. Tucking his shirt back in, he forced himself to realize what a useless turn his life had taken. He had mistaken being a dangerous man in a dangerous world with being a frontiersman in a reckless world. The difference was clear now, and he would never make such a mistake again.

Yes, he promised himself, when the noose slipped from his neck and he was put on a fast horse with a bulging saddlebag full of U.S. currency, he'd make his way south through the winter toward Mexico. But he'd detour and visit Oklahoma first. He'd head toward Fort Sill, and Geronimo.

Chapter Eight

John Stain held the crystal glassware by its delicate stem, rolling it between his fingers, watching the amber liquid inside flow nearly to the edge, then roll back upon itself. The brandy had been poured from one of six bottles imported from France three years earlier and tucked away in the dry potato cellar behind Stain's home. This bottle, the third to be opened, had been a little less full than the previous two, and Stain greatly anticipated the possibility of a slight difference of taste attributable to the liquid's years-long reaction with the trapped iota of extra air.

Stain had learned long ago that the potent libation needed to be gently swirled in order to release its distinctive delicious bouquet. He also found this preparation, the near religious adherence to this rite, to be as satisfying as the liquor itself.

He raised the glass to eye level and peered intently, allowing the bright light of the lantern sitting on his desk to burst through the crystal and give its contents the appearance of mellow fire. Satisfied, he brought the crystal to his lips and took a gentle sip, permitting the brandy to course its way across his palate and gently burn its way through his system.

Sighing contentedly, he leaned back in the ox-blood-colored leather desk chair, listening to its familiar squeaks and groans. He held the crystal in both hands, resting them against his waistcoat, and gazed deep into the brandy, forcing himself to think about both the petty problems and political realities connected with the Tom Horn affair.

How he had loved the irony behind Horn's adherence to the code of the cowboy, the dogged determination not to implicate his friends or employers in the trouble that faced him. Stain and the others had been fools not to have realized that the so-called code would be quickly amended the minute the jury allowed the judge to sentence Horn to his doom. In Horn's position, he decided, he would have done the same thing.

He knew the situation was being addressed in far too inadequate a manner. Clay Stephens's plan was inventive, all right, and even contained an element of schoolyard fun, he supposed. The conspiracy was delicious with its faked hanging, cashed-stuffed saddlebag, and dash to Mexico. It made for a wonderful story, and that's just what it would become, Stain understood. Tom Horn was not the kind of man to lay low in some *hacienda* for the rest of his years. He had roamed at will his entire life. When he wasn't on the prairie, scouting or hunting, he was in the saloons, bragging about his colorful escapades. It was precisely because he was the genuine article, the real frontiersman, that he was so dangerous. His boasts and bragging carried the weight of truth. As Stain knew, Horn, indeed, had led the life of a Western legend, and most of his braggadocio was based on fact. Stain could well imagine the scene months or years down the road when Horn decided to tie one on. He would wind up holding court in some bar in El Paso or Billings or Sacramento, throwing money around and revealing his identity as the famed gunman whose hanging had been faked. He would talk about his exploits and eventually find some newspaperman to spill his life's story to.

No, the problem had to be addressed now.

When Stephens unveiled the plan to the cattlemen the day before, Stain had remained uncharacteristically quiet. He had previously read Horn's note to the gathering, then demanded action of some sort. Then Stephens came up with his magician's trick. Stain knew something about the scheme bothered him greatly, but was somewhat cowed by the other men's enthusiasm. No one wanted Tom Horn to die, although he supposed it wouldn't have bothered him one way or the other. The fake hanging seemed a fine way to salve pained consciences.

Later, as he sat with Ford in the parlor of the ex-governor's great house after the others had left, it came to him. It seemed that those involved had forgotten their businesses—their very lives—were threatened by a single drunken cowboy. They were not unconscionable men. They saw themselves as pragmatists who occasionally had to put some business in order. Over the years, Horn had nearly become one of them, and they had certainly used him to their best advantage. Getting rid of him was one thing. Hanging him was another.

After discussions with Ford that had reached well into the early morning hours, Stain had quietly summoned several of the most influential of the cattlemen to his house that evening for what he termed an emergency meeting. They would be arriving in minutes, all except Coble, who would be conspicuous by his absence. But then, the stratagem that Stain planned to unveil could not work with Coble's knowledge. The man was just too close to Horn.

A half hour later, Stain, Peter Cooper, Frank Webster, Dave James, and Cleve Polk sat on velvet-covered chairs in Stain's library and office. They had removed their coats and stomped the snow from their boots on a thick mat in the foyer. Stain's wife had carefully hung the heavy winter coats on a rack near the door.

All except James held brandy-filled crystal. In failing health, the old cattle baron's constitution could not abide alcohol. He did, however, avail himself of one of Stain's potent cigars, lighting the tobacco with a flourish and puffing up a storm.

Stain had banished his wife and daughter to an upstairs room after they had properly greeted the guests. When he was sure they were out of earshot, he asked the group to be seated. After brief small talk and the pouring of the brandy, he stood near an ornately shaded lamp in the corner and addressed the room.

"Gentlemen. I apologize for calling you out two nights in a row in this fearsome weather, but I felt it was imperative. Governor Ford and I came to a conclusion last evening that is at odds with the decision we made when we were all together. Let me explain."

"John, where's John Coble?" interjected Pete Cooper. His long frame was plopped uncomfortably in one of the stiff velvet chairs, and he seemed in no mood for the gathering.

"John is absent because I don't believe he would appreciate what we're about to discuss. And, if you gentlemen agree with the conclusion Governor Ford and I reached, you'll understand why he's not here."

Stain had their attention now, as each fielded individual uneasiness concerning the absence of their friend. Conspiracy was certainly in the air, and they had lived long enough in intriguing times to understand the importance of being on the winning side.

"I think we need to discuss the Horn strategy in more

depth," Stain continued. "After careful thought, Ford and I reached the conclusion that the plan we endorsed last evening may well be unworkable."

"Why?" Cleve Polk interjected, his cheeks burning red from the brandy. The richest of the cattle barons, with business interests that reached from Europe to California, his folksy manner belied his steely ambition. "I thought we all understood that springing Tom from the trap was the best way to go about this business. What choice do we have? He's been down the trail. He won't cause us trouble once he crosses the Mexican border."

"That's where we differ in opinion, Cleve," said Stain. "We've all known Horn for quite a few years, and we all were . . . well, upset with the fate he endured. Then, the letter. . . ."

Stain paused to let the men think once more about the blackmail they were undergoing. Certainly they felt cowardly about letting Horn take a fall, but he'd killed Kels Nickell's kid, after all, hadn't he?

"The mere fact that Horn was in on some of the actions that had to be taken, over the past years, is unfortunate. Perhaps that's a bad choice of words, because it was certainly a fortunate thing to have both him and LeFors out on the range, subduing rustlers. We all know that."

"John, we discussed all this last night," said Dave James in a weary voice. "I think I know where you're goin' here, so just tell us."

"Fine, Dave," Stain said. He slowly looked around the room and took on the aspect of a lawyer addressing a jury. "There is no way we can allow Horn to walk away, to Mexico or otherwise. Here is a man whose entire life has been built around his frontier persona. He's created a legend featuring himself as some kind of Wild West hero.

Each of you know him well enough. He lives in a world that has disappeared.

"We needed him and we used him. We may feel bad about it, but it's something that was done to save our industry and save our state. But the mere fact that he's blackmailing us now means he'll do it again later."

Frank Webster cleared his throat and, fidgeting with his glass, said: "I've known Tom since we first sent for him. He worked for me, remember. What makes you think he'd cause us harm once he's on his way?"

"It's precisely because I *do* know him that I think so," answered Stain. "How many of you have heard about Tom showing up in the saloons and bragging about his exploits? Everyone, right? Hell, Frank, he bragged to LeFors about shooting the kid!"

The men exchanged stares at the mention of Joe LeFors.

"Well, John," said Webster in a halting tone of voice, "that's somethin' most of us have wondered about. We've not asked you about the rumors that it was you and Ford who hired Tom to go after Kels Nickell, but there's many, both cattlemen and otherwise, think that's the case."

Stain sputtered, then quickly answered: "I can assure you, Frank, that no deal was ever struck. If it existed, it existed in Horn's mind, only."

Pressing, Webster set his glass on a maple table and folded his hands over his ample belly. "I'm glad to hear that, John, because there's many who think . . . and you've heard this, I know . . . that you had somethin' to do with the killin' of the kid. I don't want to insult you, not here in your own home, but the rumor's thick as fleas out there that the kid was killed to frame Horn, and for no other reason."

Stain's jaw twitched in anger as he slugged down his brandy and turned to face Webster. "I *am* offended, Frank, to be charged so in my own home."

He tried to return Webster's flat stare and found he could not. Breaking the gaze, he said angrily: "Once again, I'll tell you all that Horn met with Governor Ford and me concerning Kels Nickell's movement of sheep on lands under our interest. After a short discussion, the governor dismissed him. Horn was not hired to kill anybody, certainly not that boy. Not that many of us wouldn't have preferred Nickell to be sent packing. Hell, we've used Horn and others to do just that to a lot of sheepmen, now, haven't we?"

Dave James smiled ironically and took another huge puff of the cigar. He looked at Webster and raised his eyebrows, waiting for him to continue.

"It's a question that had to be asked, John," replied Webster. His attitude belied the fact that he was unconvinced, but he had at least raised the specter that most of his companions had shied from. "Most of us wanted to ask it during Tom's trial, but we must not have been courageous enough. I'm glad you set us straight. Barring any reason for it, that question won't be asked again."

Stain nodded at the cattleman and made a mental note to consider the possibilities of spreading some venom that might wind up stinging Webster. But for now, he had other business.

"It comes down to this," Stain went on. "We cannot let Horn go, even under the circumstances outlined by Clay Stephens." He looked dramatically around the room, his chin uplifted, and allowed the statement to sink in.

"So what'll we do, John?" said James. "Let him hang and let the accusations make their way to the law in Denver?"

"No, of course not, Dave," answered Stain. "But I think I do have a plan. If we allow Horn his freedom, he'll turn up in a year in a Denver jail, or wind up touring with Bill Cody or some such thing. He'll brag and bluster about his days as a stock detective and how he saw the light after his deceitful employers framed him for the killing of a child."

The men around the room absorbed Stain's words, and their absolute truth struck the group as one. Setting his cigar on a tin ash plate, James said: "I see what you mean. Tom does have a flair for drama. He's smart, awright, and not prone to talk. But whisky has a tendency to loosen the tightest tongue. And I believe Tom does have a fondness for strong spirits."

"It seems like we're back between a rock and a hard spot," said Cooper. "You said you and Ford had come up with some plan. Spit it out."

Stain smiled at Cooper's bluntness and continued. "Actually I think it's a continuation of Clay's plan. We just need to play along and let Horn out of the trap. Everything can go according to plan. We'll stage the hanging, slip Horn out a few miles to Coble's spread, show him the money, and give him a horse. When he thinks he's free . . ."—Stain paused for effect—"we'll have to kill him."

James laughed out loud and said: "You mean we save his sorry rear just so's we can shoot him on the prairie?"

"Precisely," answered Stain.

"Why?" persisted James.

"Don't you see it, Dave?" Stain implored. "Horn says he's given someone evidence that will incriminate us. Once that someone thinks Horn has slipped the noose, the danger may well be over. The only person who can harm us then is Horn himself.

"Of course, we have to work with Clay Stephens to iden- tify who may be holding the information. He's busy trying to recall each and every person who's had contact with

Horn since he's been jailed. But it's my guess that, even if we don't find this mysterious person, he'll think Horn is in Mexico, living on our money. By the time he finds out different, I trust we'll have found him."

"And *I* trust you're ready to pull the trigger yourself," said Webster flatly.

"If need be, yes," said Stain.

"On Horn and his confidant?"

Stain hesitated, then said: "I won't speculate, Frank. But I know we'll all come to some acceptable consensus. We always do."

The conversation came to a stop as the men absorbed the conversation that had just occurred. Webster stood and walked to the table where the brandy bottle stood. He unstopped the cork, helped himself to three fingers, and immediately downed it. He winced from the liquor's power, brought the thumb and fingers of his left hand together over his eyes to wipe away the brandy-induced moisture, and said: "I see the necessity clearly, John, and I'll think about it. I'm frankly concerned about Horn's implications and who may have them. Killing Tom may shut him up, but I'm worried he may speak from the grave."

The rest of the assemblage mumbled consent, and even Stain nodded his agreement.

Dave James moaned as he stood, his knees weakened from nearly seventy years in the saddle. "I'll sleep on it, John," he said. "I was quick last night to buy into Clay's plan to save Tom's life. I still feel the same, but I see where you're going."

Cooper also rose and said, "I see why you didn't invite Coble. If we go through with this, we just can't let him know. He thinks too much of Horn. They're friends and he'd let it slip. If we all agree, we have to make him believe

Horn's gonna be sprung and on his way to Mexico.

"Boys, I'm with Dave. I'm gonna sleep on it. Let's meet at the hotel in the mornin' . . . in the daylight . . . and see if we can face ourselves."

After the group left, Stain sat quietly in his office. The lamps were dimmed, and he slowly puffed on a cigar, allowing the piquant smoke to caress his senses. He still burned from Webster's accusations, was still sensitive from such a close brush with the truth. As he sat back into the padded velvet chair, he remembered back to the meeting that started the whole affair, had started this house of cards folding.

Chapter Nine

It was an unusually gray and humid day in early July, 1901. The weather was a welcome reprieve from the burning sun and blistering wind that summer had brought to southern Wyoming. The humidity in the air seemed odd, and the ever-present wind was harnessed, a mere gentle breeze.

Ford and Stain had received intelligence from a number of sources concerning the incursion of sheep onto land in which one or the other of them had an interest. On that cool July day, they made a decision to take action.

Up to this point, they had sent out a number of warnings to the sheepmen, stopping short of threats. However, the sheep ranchers and homesteaders had grown bolder over the past few years, and most had even turned to rustling cattle.

Kels Nickell was foul tempered, intractable, boorish, and loud. His chiseled face and flashing eyes caused fear in those who didn't know him and that suited him just fine. His ranch near Iron Mountain was a sorry sort of thing, fit only for a little dry-land farming and a cow or two. It was exactly the sort of place the cattlemen disdained.

From the time he served under George Crook's command, fighting at the battle of the Rosebud and chasing down Sioux and Cheyennes following the battle on the Greasy Grass in 1876, Nickell had never met a man he didn't challenge or anger, and he operated by the seat of his pants. In the late 1890s, he began raising sheep on his ranch, and most likely off, as well. He raised them for a variety of reasons. Chief among them was the fact that it royally pissed off everyone. He ignored the several veiled warnings from cattle interests that came his way, angrily telling everyone within shouting distance that no rich sons-a-bitches could run him off his land. By God, if they tried, he'd kill them all.

Nickell and his family fought constantly with his neighbor, Jim Miller and his family. Bad blood is definitely thicker than water, and the blood between Nickell and Miller was of the worst kind. Their children fought at every opportunity, and they nearly came to violence innumerable times.

Like most men with reckless natures, Nickell also had a side that was hidden to most people. The rashness disappeared when he gazed at any of his nine children, and he made certain to ingrain the importance of intelligence and education into each of them. His children always came first.

When Nickell's tongue became characteristically loose, he said some foolhardy things, often the wrong things. The cattlemen could look away no longer when he declared that he would loose his sheep on neighboring property in order to "eat it off." There was precious little forage on the Wyoming prairie as it was, and allowing sheep to destroy the roots of prairie grasses was something any cattleman in the West would vow to stop.

They knew action was necessary when Nickell entered into an argument with John Coble out on the prairie and, as Coble turned away, knifed him in the stomach. Coble nearly died and had to make Tom Horn promise not to kill Nickell, at least not yet. It would do the cattle interests no good to have Coble on his deathbed and Horn in jail for murder, he said. He merely postponed the inevitable.

On that wet July day, John Stain entered Governor Ford's office fifteen minutes before Tom Horn was to meet with them. The two men reviewed their reasoning, and decided to play the meeting by ear, to see how it would go.

When Horn knocked softly on the door, Ford called for him to enter. He stood up from his desk and shook Horn's hand, as did Stain. Horn hung his hat on the rack inside the door and turned to face the men.

"Sit down, Tom," Ford said in his deep baritone. He unconsciously wiped his hand on his trousers, thinking that Horn's dry, easy grip seemed somehow reptilian. He quickly stopped when he realized the others were watching him. He promptly flexed his hand several times, smiled at Horn and Stain, and said: "Rheumatism, I'm afraid. My hand sometimes balls up like a piece of Colorado marble."

He saw the two men nod in sympathy, and congratulated himself on his quick recovery. Still, he subdued the urge to excuse himself and wash his hands. Horn, he admitted to himself, bothered him greatly.

A man who had managed by his wits and physical appearance, William Ford was impressive by anyone's estimation. Tall, with a shock of brilliant white hair, he resembled Andrew Jackson, and smiled inwardly at the comparison.

"Let's have a little snort, boys," he said as he reached for a bourbon bottle and glasses. He poured and handed the two men three fingers of whisky each.

"How are things out on the range, Tom?" he asked. "Are we keeping the rustlers at bay?"

Horn favored the politician with an amused expression and said: "Yes, sir, Gov'nor. I believe we're winnin' the battle. I think you've received the reports I've passed on to John Coble and John Stain, here." He cocked an eyebrow and watched as Ford nodded his agreement. "The deal we reached a couple of years ago has worked out well, I think."

"Well, I'm glad to hear that, Tom," Ford said uneasily. The earlier meeting between a suspected assassin and himself was a political risk he had to take. If he had allowed rustlers to continue to raid cattlemen's herds, including his own, his future may as well have been doomed. Action had to be taken, so he took it, with the full acknowledgement of the Wyoming Stock Grower's Association. After Horn's summons from Denver and first encounter with the cattlemen, he approved the disbursement of funds necessary to have Horn ply his particular type of detective work. The private meeting that later occurred cemented the relationship.

Of course, rumors began to fly. He had publicly denied that he and Horn had struck any sort of deal on the part of the cattle interests, and had told Horn he would do so. Horn understood perfectly. He did his job, ridding southern Wyoming and northern Colorado of a few rambunctious, wrong-headed souls, never mentioning the connection with Ford.

"Tom, I've been talking with John here about some trouble we just can't avoid any more," Ford continued. "Quite frankly, we believe the time has come to deal with Kels Nickell."

Horn snorted, actually spewing whisky through his nose. He wiped his moustache with the back of his hand. "Hell, yes," he said, his entire body animated. "The son-of-a-bitch knifed John, and I should 'a' shot him down like a dog. John couldn't see any sense in it right then. He made me promise to hold back . . . said the time would come."

"Well, so it has," said Ford.

Stain stood and walked to the governor's desk, leaning

against the corner. "Tom," he said, "everyone agrees Nickell was a marked man the moment he attacked Coble. We just couldn't afford to take action then. It was too blatant."

"I understand, and I agree," said Horn, nodding his head and tossing one arm cavalierly up and to the side. He quickly adjusted himself in the straight-backed chair and licked his lips. Speaking to Ford, he said: "Believe I could use another snort, Gov'nor. You mind?"

Ford picked up the bottle and set it on a polished mahogany table next to Horn. "Absolutely not. Whisky's for drinking, that's what they say."

"Amen," said Horn as he picked up the bottle and poured his glass nearly full. He took a good-size swig, grunted with satisfaction, then said: "You know, it's mighty curious that both Nickell and me served under General Crook. 'Course, I was in Arizona while Nickell rode with Crook up on the Rosebud. Now there was a man, awright. The finest Indian fighter and greatest gent I ever knew. I just can't figure out how a man like Nickell could serve under Crook and turn into the lowdown scum he is. It just don't make sense."

"I'm sure you're right, Tom," said Ford. "I knew Crook myself. Met him in Washington at an official function. He truly was a giant among men."

Horn nodded in appreciation and continued to sip from the glass in his hands.

Stain's contempt for small talk was well known, and he interjected himself into the conversation. "Tom, let's talk particulars. The governor and I have talked with some of the boys, and we want to make sure this is done as . . . well . . . as quietly as possible. Everyone from Iron Mountain south knows that Jim Miller and Nickell despise the ground the other walks on. I don't think it will be difficult to deflect suspicion Miller's way."

"Uhn-huh," mumbled Horn as he took another sip of the burning liquid.

In fact, Stain and Ford had not conferred with any other prominent cattlemen concerning the problem posed by Kels Nickell. Planning a murder was not something that was accomplished by committee.

Stain looked directly at Horn, pursed his lips, and said: "I understand that you have a certain . . . um . . . relationship with the schoolmarm, Miss Kimmell."

Horn's eyes bored into Stain, daring him to say the wrong thing. Stain managed to return the stare and gather the courage to give the implications in his statement a positive bent.

"Tom, you know she's staying at the Miller's spread. Once Nickell is taken care of, and Miller is under suspicion, well, I just want you to keep in mind that she's out there, that's all."

Horn sighed deeply, then stared at the floor. At length, he said: "Yeah, I'll keep that in mind."

After an awkward silence, Ford said: "Tom, John doesn't mean anything. He's just thinking about your welfare, your happiness. It may not look good for Miss Kimmell to be living in the home of a suspect in the unfortunate events that might occur."

"Well, thank you, Gov'ner," Horn said quietly, "but I think me an' the schoolmarm have little to say to each other these days. But I'll keep your concern in mind."

Horn stood and walked to the office window, noted the sky that portended a gusher, and stared into the dusty street. Already hitching posts were being torn down and a new ordinance called for all horses to be stabled. There were seven automobiles in Cheyenne, each louder and more obnoxious than the first. In fact, they rivaled the thunder that began to boom off to the west. It just wasn't the same.

He turned and said: "I hate to be blunt, boys, but I assume I won't be dealin' with Nickell as part of our general arrangement. This ain't like the others."

Ford shook his head side to side and put up his hands. "Of course not, Tom. I understand you'll require some expense money."

"Yep," said Horn. "I think five hundred dollars oughta do."

Stain's eyes widened, and he started to speak, only to be cut off by Ford. "Of course, that's more than reasonable, Tom."

Horn tossed down the last of his drink as Stain made a show out of pulling his pocket watch from his waistcoat fob and noting the time.

"Governor," he said, "I believe you need to meet with the Cheyenne town council shortly."

Ford shot Stain a grateful look and said: "Certainly, John. Thank you. Tom, is there anything else we need to discuss?"

"I don't believe so," Horn answered.

"Then we have an agreement. I'll have the cash to you soon, unless you need it immediately."

"Sooner's better than later, Gov'ner," said Horn. "But a few days'll make no difference."

"All right, then," said Ford. He cleared his throat and said: "As usual, we have no need to know of particulars. As you understand, if anyone asks or suspects us, it's best that we don't know. We trust you, Tom. You know best how to handle these situations. And Tom, this action is outside the purview of your arrangement with the Stock Growers Association. Only a few others have knowledge. I'd appreciate it if we could keep it like that."

"Absolutely, Gov'nor. It's best that way." Horn grabbed his hat from the rack and pulled it low on his head. He clicked his tongue at the men and said: "Well, boys, thank you for the vote o' confidence. I'll keep in touch."

Stain remembered Horn's walking from the office as the clouds let loose, showering rain on the dusty streets, turning them instantly into mud. It reminded him of a time in Pennsylvania when, as a nine-year-old boy, he had looked around the corner of the tiny house he and his seven brothers and sisters shared with their mother to see a man who had just visited his mother in private duck out the back door into the rain and quickly disappear down a side street into a saloon. Watching the drenched man gave him a sickly, sad feeling, and he couldn't help but feel the same as he watched Horn stop and look up at the storm, then look slowly back to the window as he made his way across the street. He waved quickly as he entered the lobby of a hotel where he would enter a poker game that had been going on for nearly two days.

He remembered seeing Kels Nickell in Cheyenne a week or so later, and wondering what Horn had in mind. That same day, he sent a messenger to Horn at Frank Webster's ranch with an envelope that contained $500 in cash.

The next thing he knew, Clay Stephens showed up at his door and told him that fourteen-year-old Willie Nickell had been shot and killed by an assassin. He was tending his father's sheep, opening a gate to a pasture, when he was shot two times. Clay was on his way up to Iron Mountain to question the Millers.

Stain thanked Stephens and told him he'd convey the information to Ford. When Stephens left, he walked to a chair in his office and sat heavily. His mind was reeling, replaying the conversation with Horn that had taken place in Ford's office barely two weeks earlier. He desperately wanted a drink, but couldn't make himself stand to fetch a bottle. *Fourteen years old,* he thought.

Later, as the particulars came in, it was known that a .30-30 was used in the murder, and that the shot came from some distance. The Millers were suspected, but had alibis. Stain thought his head would explode as he pondered the fact that Horn had used a .30-30. He pondered what purpose might have been served by the killing, but could come up with none. He could find fifty people on the streets of Cheyenne at that moment who would swear that Kels Nickell needed killing, but none would even contemplate the death of young Willie. Surely Horn wouldn't have shot the boy. He was a professional, for God's sake. Although he'd dispatched several men, he'd never been a mad-dog killer like Wes Hardin or those James boys. Stain believed that Horn had always disliked killing as much as the rest of those in the cattle business, but saw the necessity of keeping order. To Stain's knowledge, he had never killed just for the killing. Yet.

Alibis or not, it must have been Jim Miller or his boys. Nickell and Miller had a blood feud going on. In fact, Stain had heard something about fisticuffs on the prairie. It must have been the Millers, he thought. It *had to* have been the Millers, because the alternative was too upsetting to ponder.

Then, weeks later, word came that Kels Nickell had been shot and was in bad shape. This time, Horn was out of the state, most likely drinking like a fish in some Colorado saloon and contributing to some lonely whore's old age.

Clay Stephens had an inkling of the deal struck between

Ford and Horn, and asked Stain point-blank. When he got an answer he thought sounded like the truth, he let Stain know that no one west of the Mississippi in their right mind would think anyone but Tom Horn had killed the kid. It had his signature written all over it. A long shot from cover—a patient gunman—a target that was causing cattle interests a whole passel of grief. In light of Stephens's logic, it was decided that, whether Horn shot the boy or not, he was probably going to have to answer for the crime. Stain reluctantly allowed that Stephens was right, but in light of Horn's history with the cattlemen his arrest could prove disastrous. Stephens felt that Horn's reputation as a tight-lipped cowboy who betrayed no confidences would likely work in the cattlemen's favor. In fact, other than finding Horn and shooting him on sight, the assurance that Horn wouldn't talk was probably the cattlemen's best hope. Soon the two concocted a plan that called for some fancy detective work that would entrap Horn, erasing from anyone's mind the notion that he *could* be innocent of Willie Nickell's murder.

Stephens brought in Joe LeFors, who was deputized as a U.S. marshal. He sent the crusty detective out to the Nickell spread in hope of finding something. LeFors had worked for cattle interests much longer than Horn and was called in as much to reassure a boiling-mad public that something was being done as for his skills at detective work.

LeFors showed up and met with Stain and Stephens. Asked as a formality whether he thought Horn had killed Willie Nickell, LeFors let loose with a brown spew of tobacco juice and answered that it was surely a fact. But if not, it was no never mind. He said the thinking around Wyoming went something like this: Kels Nickell was shot because he deserved it, most likely. There were about as many suspects as men in the state. Willie Nickell was another situation altogether. Everything about the killing pointed to Horn.

The decision was made to have LeFors try to pry some information from Horn. But first, they had to get Horn back from Denver, where he'd been laid up. A letter from LeFors offering an opportunity to ply the stock detective trade in Montana did the trick. Horn took the bait like a hungry trout after the first snowmelt.

LeFors consequently met Horn in a Cheyenne saloon. Horn was already in his cups, glad to be shut of the troubles he'd endured in Colorado over the past months. The two had a few more shots of whisky and decided to retire to LeFors's temporary office. The resulting conversation was transcribed by Charlie Ohnhaus, who was hidden in the next room. The words on paper, sent directly to Ford and his contingent, certainly looked like a confession.

The public was in a clamor about the boy's murder, and something had to be done before things got ugly and cattle interests were blamed. The entrapment of Tom Horn was complete.

Then came Horn's arrest, the result of the drunken confession to LeFors. The trial had been a colorful mockery, its outcome predetermined. John Coble reported that Horn would honor his code of silence, that none of them had anything to worry about. Then came Horn's letter.

There was so much Stain didn't know and couldn't adequately put in perspective. For a fastidious man used to understanding even the minutiæ of any situation, the Horn circumstance was sheer torture.

Who had killed Willie Nickell? Despite Horn's conviction, Stain couldn't imagine that he had really shot the boy.

That left the Millers or, in the minds of many in southern Wyoming to whom the Johnson County War was still a recent memory, the cattlemen. Of course, as he had just found out, some of the cattlemen themselves even went so far as to suspect him and Governor Ford.

He racked his brain trying to imagine who could have shot Kels Nickell. Horn was in Denver then, it seemed, having taken a jaunt down to the saloons and getting himself in a scrape or two. Hell, he even spent three weeks in a hospital with a broken jaw he had received in a barroom brawl.

So what was going on?

Stain sighed as he rose from his chair and dimmed the lamps throughout the lower portion of the house. As he ascended the stairs to his bedroom, he couldn't stop thinking about all the loose ends that needed to be tied up.

I've got to find Horn's accomplice, he said to himself as he entered the dark bedroom to the sound of his wife's soft, regular breathing. He stood still for a moment, letting his eyes adjust to the darkness, and listened to the wind whistle through the skeletal cottonwoods and willows bordering a nearby creek.

I must find him. And I must do it now.

Chapter Ten

He supposed it was her eyes that captivated him. He'd never seen anything like them. Golden brown, with flecks of bright yellow and deep chocolate, they seemed too bottomless to fathom. When he spoke to her without making eye contact, he found her much less interesting, her droning tone of voice and superior attitude actually irritating. But when she managed to catch his gaze and hold it, he became entranced, unable to stop talking about himself, about his deeds and dreams.

Her ability to play his emotions and turn him into a fickle schoolboy was frightening to him, and all the bravado he'd practiced and perfected throughout the years vanished the moment he met her gaze. Yet, the same look could cause him to brag and bluster, to augment every adventure, and to lie like a politician.

Now, her eyes invaded the quiet privacy of his cell, and there was little he could do about it. He couldn't avoid them. They stared at him through the tiny square opening in the cell door, framed by splintered wood and rust-flecked iron bars, and her flat, Midwestern voice spoke softly in a tone that suggested both sympathy and self-pity. He felt trapped, with no recourse but to stare into those forever eyes. When he'd felt like this before the kid's death turned the world upside down, he could always shift his gaze to the velvet collar of her woolen frock, or to the golden pins holding her dark upswept hair into place. Or even, in other circumstances, to the intoxicating sight of her milk-white skin exposed to the warm Wyoming sun, so brilliant in contrast to the earth-toned saddle blanket and disheveled green dress that had been hurriedly tossed onto the rough prairie. On those occasions, the only way he could keep himself from feeling like he was floating away into the void was to break her stare and watch the pale hollow of her throat beat in delicate time to her racing heart. But now, her face filled the small aperture, and he was drawn into the eyes that made him feel enamored and inadequate at the same time. He was cornered.

"Tom," she whispered. "How are you? I mean . . . well, how *are* you?"

"As well as possible, I s'pose," he answered haltingly.

Glendolene Kimmell's eyes blazed through the opening, causing him to stammer and stutter. She was the only person in his memory who affected him this way. His reaction to her was too obvious for her not to notice, and since their first meeting she had taken good advantage of it. She knew that she affected Horn, but often wondered just how. She had asked him on dozens of occasions if she made him uncomfortable, but he always answered no. Yet, she knew she held some power over him, and satisfied herself with the very fact.

She had come to the West looking for adventure, looking for her cowboy. When she had met Tom Horn, she had stopped her search. In her view, she had chanced across a genuine legend, perhaps the last of the real frontiersmen. People spoke his name with awe. Some people loved him, others despised him, but he was always feared. She wasn't about to let him get away.

Like Horn, Glendolene Kimmell moved to the music of

a great river. Born and raised in Hannibal, Missouri, she looked upon the Mississippi as an integral part of her life. At times, since her arrival in Wyoming, she felt it course through her veins, physically compelling her to leave the high plains and return, to follow the muddy Platte on its meandering course to the wide Missouri, and on across country from St. Joe to Hannibal—on to the truly great river. At other times, she despised its hold on her, and doubled her resolve to break its chains. She craved adventure, and thought of herself as a seeker of truth, an observer of the human condition. Her education afforded her such lofty opinions, and she used her wit as a weapon against the unwashed and uneducated. She looked upon herself as a scientist among the natives, an anthropological explorer, but with a significant difference. The natives often stimulated her. As she often said, she was strongly attracted to the frontier type. She was entranced with the Western ethic, with the pioneer spirit. The only way she found to rectify her divergent impulses was to offer enlightenment. She was a schoolmarm.

She had stepped off the train at the Union Pacific station in Cheyenne one evening in July, 1901. The ride from Omaha had seemed interminable and the heat impossible. The cool evening breeze she had felt when disembarking from the train car immediately invigorated her, and she walked across the expansive boardwalk toward the station with a light step. The porter carried her valise inside, set it on an oaken bench, tipped his hat, and disappeared back into the night.

She turned around to see a mustachioed, middle-aged man examining her. Meeting his gaze, she tilted her head in a questioning fashion and favored him with a coy grin. The man smiled, removed his broad-brimmed hat, and walked toward her. The sound of his boot steps meeting the worn hardwood floor echoed throughout the room, eclipsing even the furious steam of the idling engine outside.

"Pardon me, ma'am. You would be Miss Kimmell?"

"Why, yes, sir, I am Glendolene Kimmell. And you must be Mister John Coble."

John Coble smiled even wider and reached out to shake the young woman's hand. His initial assessment had been surprise at the confident manner in which she held herself. Now, as he grasped the gloved hand that returned his firm pressure, he knew he had just met a young woman with exceptional spirit.

"John Coble I am, miss. But I'm less certain about the title of *Mister* you've so kindly favored me with." Both of them chuckled, and Coble found himself enchanted with her sweet laughter.

"We're delighted to have you. And meeting you now, I must say the children of Iron Mountain have chanced into a piece of luck."

Her laughter echoed through the station.

"Why, thank you, sir," she said as she met his eyes with a direct stare. "It's been a long journey, but your kind heart makes it all worthwhile."

Coble chuckled under his breath and thought to himself that they had hired a high-spirited woman, all right. This one was out to break a heart or two.

John Coble had sent for her on the recommendation of a Cheyenne schoolmarm who had chanced to run into the young woman on a visit to Missouri. At a reception for her sister's wedding, the schoolmarm found herself seated next to a vivacious young woman. As they began to talk, the woman allowed that she was also a teacher, and was fascinated with the whole idea of the West. She peppered the schoolmarm with questions about Wyoming, about Cheyenne, and about Iron Mountain. She asked about the mountains and plains, about the frontier ethic, and about the cowboys who rode the range. She talked of the fascination that had overtaken her as she learned about the frontier while in school. An hour later, filled with information from the schoolmarm, Miss Kimmel asked about the children, and if there was need for yet another teacher.

The schoolmarm returned to Wyoming and told John Coble that a certain Miss Kimmell had expressed a desire to see the West, and to engage in adventure. One of the teachers at Iron Mountain had recently married a ranch foreman and moved off near Jackson Hole, so finding her replacement was, indeed, a priority. When Coble wrote to Glendolene Kimmell with a proposal to come to Wyoming as one of the schoolmarms for the Iron Mountain community, she immediately wired back her acceptance. She packed a valise, kissed her parents on their cheeks, and jumped on the next westbound train.

She and Coble talked incessantly on the wagon ride from the depot to her temporary quarters in the home of Jim Miller and his family. Long before, she had come to recognize and utilize her ability to loosen tongues. Coble proved to be no match for her. He talked about the cattle business, and gave her a run-down on the Johnson County fracas of a few years earlier, where no one won and everyone lost. He talked about Pennsylvania, and summer nights in the Appalachians as a child. He told her about the English and Scots who had owned nearly all of southern Wyoming and northern Colorado at one time. He told her everything.

For her part, she listened and absorbed, occasionally throwing in an observation or comment concerning her life. She let Coble know that her family had means, although they were certainly not of society. Her father had been a sea captain, she allowed, a severe German whose sea legs took him up the wide Mississippi after a life of exploring the oceans. He had taken a wife in Taipei, a woman of mixed Anglo and Oriental blood. The extraordinary combination resulted in a daughter with bottomless eyes, a Siren, her father said. She attributed her own wanderlust to that of her father. He had explored the Seven Seas. She would explore the continent.

The enchanted Coble filled her in on local customs and personalities and delivered her to the home of Jim Miller and his family, where she would be staying until adequate housing could be built. When she was settled into the little room inside the Miller home, she thanked Coble and watched as his buggy left the dusty yard and settled onto the deeply rutted road that led back toward Cheyenne. She felt immense regret that she had not asked him to stay longer.

She had been in Wyoming only a matter of months, living in the tiny room at the Miller family's house, when she realized her ambition. She was deflated, feeling utterly deceived by the windswept expanse of Wyoming. Her search for adventure and the rugged frontier had turned into a mundane existence of attempting to teach the ABCs to snot-nosed ranch kids who smelled of sheep and coughed dust from their lungs constantly. She had to put up with the unfailing stares from the males on the Miller spread, stares that suggested more than a casual tip of the hat. It wasn't that she couldn't handle these men. She could. She was merely frustrated that such attention came from shepherds and fence menders who bathed about as often as they used proper English.

She had come to find the romance of the West, and instead found only the constant wind that soared across a rock-hard land. There was no intrigue; there was only disappointment. She found the people of Iron Mountain boring and stupid, and began to question her decision to come to so desolate a place. She thought that perhaps Colorado or California would be better.

Then she attended the barn dance.

The entire community had prepared for the festivities at Frank Webster's spread for over a month. Pies were baked, roasts were prepared, and musicians were contracted. The immense barn loft had been spotlessly cleaned for the affair, and would remain so for a week or two until it was once again filled with hay and grain. Nearly two hundred people milled in and around the barn, the women serving food and talking as the men walked back and forth from the barn to the hidden stash of sour mash behind the granary. It was a time to catch up, a time to find out if the wind had driven anyone loco during the hard winter.

Glendolene Kimmell made the rounds, talking with the women and ostensibly committing recipes and folk cures to memory. When the music began in the loft, she was escorted up the steep stairway by John Coble. A few couples danced to slow waltzes while others sat on straight-backed chairs. She couldn't help wincing at the inevitable smell of livestock that permeated the barn, but was soon used to it.

She had just finished politely declining the invitation to dance from the tipsy father of seven of her students when she looked out through the haymow, down into the yard, and noticed a rider lope up to the barn. A tall man with a light brown moustache and silverbelly Stetson, he rode like he was part of the animal, with a smooth, supine grace that defied most men. She was immediately intrigued, and asked

John Coble the rider's identity.

"Why, that's Tom Horn, miss. I believe you know of him."

Indeed, she did. Since she had stepped off the train in Cheyenne, she had heard of little else. Tom Horn was a dangerous man, it was intimated. He was a former Indian fighter and perhaps the country's finest rifle shot. He could break any broncho and ride any four-legged animal on the range. He also did the cattlemen's dirty work.

When Horn had dismounted and climbed to the loft to talk with Coble, Glendolene Kimmell openly assessed him. His clothing was nearly new and very clean, no doubt for this occasion. His lean frame was appealing, as was his height. At 6'3", he towered over Coble and virtually everyone else in attendance. His moustache carried the slightest hint of gray, as did the hair at his temples that was visible from beneath the cowboy hat. His entire demeanor seemed to her to capture the essence of the West.

When Coble walked Horn over to meet her, she saw that he was nervous. She found it immediately endearing that a man who was as close to a legend as it got in these parts was somehow shy around women, or at least around her. She liked him immediately.

"Miss Glendolene Kimmell," Coble said, "I'd like you to meet Tom Horn."

"Miss Kimmell," said Horn as he removed his hat and nodded his head. He held her gaze for an instant before seeming to stare at the tops of his boots.

"Hello, Mister Horn," she said. "I've been hearing much about you."

He seemed aghast as he took a quick peek toward Coble. "I . . . I hope what you've heard isn't, well, disturbing, miss."

"Of course not," she said. "I understand you're one of the last of the true cowboys."

"Perhaps," he said, staring at the hat in his hands. "That could be true, I s'pose. There ain't many left from the old days. 'Course, I was younger than most then."

She smiled and reached out to grab Horn's arm, siding up to him. Looking up at the astonished cowboy, she locked eyes and said: "I'd like to hear about your life, about the cowboy's life." Without pausing, she began to walk, pulling him with her, saying: "It's very stuffy up here. Shall we walk about the grounds?"

Horn nodded and said: "If you mean Webster's barnyard, we shall, indeed."

He walked the woman to the near-vertical staircase and held her hand while she descended. He thought she had a fine grip. As they walked out of the barn and began to stroll in the afternoon sun, she said: "I understand you work with John . . . Coble, that is. He seems to put much stock in you."

"Well, yes, miss, and the feelin's mutual," said Horn while steering her toward the shade of a large old cottonwood. "John was the one brought me up here from Denver a few years back to help out with some of the troubles they had goin' on with rustlers and such. I'd been floatin' around between New Mexico and Colorado, and didn't rightly know what I'd do next. When we met, I knew right off I'd found a good friend, and a good friend he is. John's a man to ride the trail with."

She was thrilled by the Western vernacular that peppered Horn's speech, and thought she caught a glimpse of something deeper than a simple range hand. True friendship was a Western value, she understood. Now she had the opportunity to perceive it in action.

"I tend to agree, although I've only known him for a few months," she said. She paused briefly, then said: "I'm an observer, Mister Horn. I love to observe people, and I think I'm good at sensing what moves them and makes them do the things they do. If I'm not being forward, I'd like to observe you more closely. I believe you are a fascinating man."

Horn's face was nearly the color of his bright red bandanna as he sputtered: "Well, of course, miss, I wouldn't mind . . . well, you know."

"Please, call me Myrt," she interjected. "That is, if I can call you Tom."

"Well, of course," he said. "But . . . why do they call you Myrt?"

"Because, *Tom* . . . my middle name is Myrtle," she teased, and let loose a peal of laughter that caused Horn to guffaw himself.

Within a few weeks they were lovers, with Horn stopping by the schoolhouse regularly while on his rounds throughout the cattlemen's domain. They would ride out onto the endless prairie in one of Coble's buckboards and eat the cold sandwiches she had packed, all the while chatting and contentedly staring at the vast expanse of Western sky. She would caress his face with her small hands, and draw out his stories and memories of the frontier, of a time that seemed the most exciting in the history of the world.

It was on one of these sojourns to the country that she prompted him to tell her about Cuba. Under the magic of that stare he'd added a few revised facts and fantasies to the story, but it was mainly the truth. Even if it was enamored a bit, it had still happened. It was still real.

Chapter Eleven

In the cool Wyoming wind, what he remembered most was the heat, the smothering, swarming heat of the Caribbean. He'd known heat before, in Arizona, but it was a dry heat that was gone as soon as night fell. Cuba was a different story, a muggy swamp of a place, not the paradise he had expected.

He'd never really felt bothered by the line of work he practiced in Wyoming. He didn't believe in ghosts, and devoutly felt that those he dispatched for his employers deserved it. Yet, something was eating at him. Twice, he swore he saw Fred Powell loping across the prairie on a brown mare a couple of miles down the Chugwater Slope. Each time was a shock, as he had shot and killed Powell from ambush three years earlier. He had watched a geyser of blood explode from the man's chest and had walked up and turned the body over on its back with his boot. He tried to follow the mysterious rider, both times losing him near Horse Creek, where Powell had settled and died.

He shrugged the sightings off, attributing them either to bad whisky or questionable eyesight. Then, one night as he stepped out the rear door of a favorite Cheyenne watering hole to relieve himself, he saw someone standing on the other side of the railroad tracks, fifty or sixty yards away. Squinting, he walked unsteadily toward the shadowy figure. It immediately began moving down a bank leading toward the river, but not before the moonlight revealed it to be Bill Lewis. Horn felt the hair raise on the back of his neck as he thought of carefully sighting down the barrel of his .30-30 Winchester and firing off the fatal slugs that had killed the rustler back in 1895. His stomach nearly revolted as he tried to absorb the shock of seeing the dead man retreating in front of him. Gaining courage born of rotgut whisky, he reeled after the figure, only to slip and stumble down the loose crushed rock that lined the grade. He rolled to a stop near a discarded rail tie and slowly sat up, taking inventory of his scrapes and bruises. Realizing that his trousers were shredded, he stood and looked angrily around, swaying back and forth in the wind from both fear and whisky. There, in the moonlight, nearly a half mile away, a lone figure walked in the opposite direction.

"You god-damn' Cockney!" Horn screamed after the figure. "You got what you deserved, you English bastard."

He stood in the darkness, looking after the figure until a train began moving from the station, throwing its light on him. He quickly scampered up the bank and back into the bar where he glared at anyone who looked as if they might question his tattered clothing and scraped hands.

The next week Horn signed on as a civilian employee of the Army and was on his way to Tampa, Florida to take part in supplying troops engaged in fighting the Spanish in Cuba. He went to John Coble and told him he needed to see other country for a while. He figured his knowledge of the Spanish tongue and of horseflesh would be welcome in the Caribbean campaign. He was right. Coble wired a captain in Washington D.C. who was an acquaintance with a request that Horn be considered for civilian duty as an interpreter and horseman. Six hours later, the request was fulfilled. Horn was put on immediately and wired a ticket for passage from Wyoming to Florida.

The long train ride was made bearable by several bottles of Kentucky's finest, and he remembered little of the transit other than the rhythm of the rails. Twice he thought he felt someone across the aisle staring at him, but when he looked, he saw only a sleeping salesman and a dark-garbed crone staring straight ahead. A day out from his destination, he decided it would be propitious to arrive sober, so he concentrated on both food and the countryside.

He had hightailed it out of Wyoming to dodge a couple of ghosts, he figured, so he was shocked to his core when he walked off the train only to meet with what seemed to be yet another apparition. There, standing under the station's portico, leaning against the brick wall with his arms folded across his chest and a mischievous grin on his face, stood Edward Plummer. Laughing at Horn's surprise, Plummer pushed off from the wall, stood, and straightened his uniform.

"By God, you're a sight fer sore eyes, Lieutenant," bellowed Horn as he rushed across the shaded area.

Meeting him halfway, Plummer grabbed his hand and pumped it wildly. "So are you, Tom, so are you. But it's Captain Plummer these days."

Horn shook his head in disbelief at meeting his old friend so far from the West. Letting go of the other man's hand, he said: "I lost track of you after you took off to Fort Union, then I heard you was back to Fort Sill, lordin' it up over Geronimo and such."

"Well, this man's army does move you around, Tom. I know I've got a family somewhere, I just don't believe they've caught up with me. Geronimo and his Apaches don't pose much of a threat these days, do they? But the Spanish certainly do. Which is why we're both here."

"Both?" queried Horn.

"Yes, sir, Tom. I met Colonel Roosevelt when he was out West, shooting bears and such, and we've managed to stay in touch. When this Spanish affair began in Cuba, he asked for me proper. I've been here going on a year as base adjutant and supply officer." Plummer gave a playful laugh. "When I heard through the wire that the great scout and cowboy Tom Horn was on his way down to defeat the god-forsaken Spaniards his ownself, I decided I needed him in my company. Which is why I'm here to meet you."

Horn scratched his head and thought about the whole affair. "Life's sure big on catchin' you with yer britches down when you least expect it," he said. "Most o' the surprises I get, I hate. This one makes up fer all the others."

The two men walked off to a waiting carriage that took them to Plummer's quarters. Over mess, they talked about the old days on the frontier, and questioned each other as to the whereabouts of old friends and companions. Plummer asked Horn about his business, what he'd been up to.

"Well, Ed, I'm workin' fer livestock interests outta Cheyenne. Have been fer a few years now. I'm what's called a stock detective, meanin' I hunt down lost cattle . . . mostly cattle that've been lost on purpose, I 'spect. There's still a bunch a cattle thievin' goin' on up through Wyomin' and Montana. I'm just tryin' to stop it, that's all."

Plummer looked at Horn and saw the strain on the man's face. Kindly he said: "There's no excuse for stealing another man's property, that's for sure." Then, changing course, he continued: "You know, Tom, change is a rough thing. Hell, I've been through change my whole life, moving from post to post, and I expect it'll be that way till they put me under. It must be hard on you to know the Old West isn't there any longer. I believe we experienced its death throes nearly fifteen years ago."

Horn nodded in agreement.

"That's why Geronimo finally gave up, you know," Plummer continued. "He told me. We had plenty of time to sit around and gossip at Fort Sill. Not much else to do in that country. He told me it wasn't just the Indians whose way of life was gone. It was all of us. You, me, Sieber, Crook . . . all of us. He said our time was past."

Plummer sighed and stared at the half-eaten food before him. "He was absolutely right. All the adventure we hoped for . . . hell, that *you* lived for . . . was gone overnight. It's just like they turned out a light, isn't it? All of a sudden, the Wild West wasn't there any more."

He glanced at Horn, who favored him with a sad smile.

"I suppose I've been lucky enough to have a profession that keeps me moving around," he continued. "I know it must be rough on you to ride the West and see everything so . . ."—he hesitated for a moment, searching for the right word—"so, well, *civilized*."

Horn raised his hand to stop Plummer, and said: "Ah, now, Ed, don't be cryin' no tears fer me. I'm still a pretty young fella with a lotta livin' left to do."

Both men laughed and thought how good the old memories felt, even the painful ones. Horn took a swig from a bottle of beer, wiped his mouth with the back of his hand, and said: "Things have changed, all right. There's no doubt. But I don't mind civilization too much. Denver's a bit too big for my taste, but the Wyomin' prairie is still a pretty wide-open place. I can still at least *feel* like I'm lost on occasion."

Later, Plummer gave Horn his orders. Sitting on the verandah of the quarters, safely ensconced behind mosquito netting, Plummer said: "I'm charged with putting together the supplies for Colonel Roosevelt to mount an all-out attack on the Spanish. We'll have everything together by Wednesday, and we sail Thursday. I want you to be with me to translate at first. When we arrive in Cuba, there'll be fighting, I expect."

When they docked in Cuba, Plummer's troops immediately unloaded nearly six hundred mules and began packing them with provisions. Many of the mules actually had to be pushed into the water when they refused to walk down the gangplank. Horn assured the skeptical soldiers that the mules could swim to shore with no problem. With no other option, Plummer ordered the mules dumped, causing confusion to reign briefly as soldiers chased down soggy pack animals emerging from the sea.

As the supply train was being readied, Plummer and Horn mounted two of the very few Army horses on the island and rode to a military bivouac on the beach. Dismounting, Plummer saluted a sentry stationed before a large canvas tent, then entered through the upraised flap with Horn in tow.

"Colonel," he said, addressing the man sitting at the maple desk. He then saluted.

Colonel Theodore Roosevelt fairly jumped from his camp stool. "At ease, Captain, at ease," he said as he rushed around the desk. Standing directly in front of Plummer and Horn, he excitedly said: "I take it we will have adequate supplies for our endeavor?"

"Yes, sir," answered Plummer. "Some of the mules got a little frisky, but they should be packed and ready to go in no time. Colonel Roosevelt, this is Tom Horn, a *compañero* of mine, from my days in Arizona."

Roosevelt shook Horn's hand with his characteristic verve, all the while looking at Plummer, no doubt wanting him to explain Horn's presence.

"Tom's an expert interpreter. He knows Spanish, all right. Plus, he can figure out just about any dialect. In fact, Geronimo calls him Talking Boy. Tom was pretty near the only white man the old chief would talk to, outside of George Crook. He also knows horses better than any man I've ever met."

Satisfied, Roosevelt looked at Horn and said: "Captain Plummer's recommendation is high praise, indeed. Geronimo's, also, I'm sure. We'll have some excitement down here with these Spaniards, Mister Horn. Welcome to the fray."

Before Horn could answer, Roosevelt had bounded back behind the desk and beckoned Plummer forward. For the next two hours, Horn watched the man animatedly pour over maps and intelligence reports, giving Plummer a quick education into the strategy that would be employed in meeting the Spanish. Horn excused himself and walked out of the tent, intending to find the latrine. As he walked along the beach, he was amazed at the absolute color of the place. He had spent his life since leaving Missouri in the West, amid the browns and pastels of the deep cañons and blues of the high mountains. Absorbing the deep green of the island's vegetation combined with the bone white beach and crystal hues of the ocean itself made Horn feel like a blind man who had been granted vision. Yet, as he continued to walk and grow more used to the lushness, he reckoned that what the West lacked in color, it made up for in character. Used to the wide-open spaces of Wyoming, he felt nervous as he examined the thick line of trees that hid the island's interior. All in all, he felt that Cuba was probably just a pretty, flat spot surrounded by water. In the end, it made him feel constrained. He felt confused by the course his life had taken, and relentlessly pursued by his virtues and vices alike. Like Cuba, he thought he might be floundering in the middle of the ocean.

In the following weeks, Horn observed Roosevelt to be a man of boundless energy and nearly insufferable excitement. A consummate outdoorsman and connoisseur of horseflesh, the colonel engaged Horn on several occasions in discussions concerning the merits of various horses. He also had Horn work as an interpreter with Cuban nationals dedicated to fighting the Spanish, picking their brains for possible strategies and eventually contributing to overall American intelligence efforts.

Roosevelt was constantly surrounded by his troops, who proudly adopted the colonel's designation of Rough Riders. They were the best horsemen Horn had seen since his days in Apache country, although horses were at a premium, with most being left in Tampa. Proud to the point of arrogance, they exhibited their commander's bravado and itched to enter into battle.

After several days, Horn's feelings of disassociation began to wane, and he found himself thinking less and less of the moral dichotomies that faced him on the open prairie of Wyoming and Colorado. His ghosts had been put to rest, he reckoned, as he immersed himself in the strategies of supplying an invading army.

Working with loyal Cubans, he and Plummer mapped out potential supply routes, constantly playing devil's advocate in their need to anticipate every contingency. Then the fighting began.

Roosevelt led his troops inland, engaging the enemy at various points across the eastern end of the island. Plummer saw that food and ammunition were in constant supply as the Americans marched their way toward Spanish fortifications. He was at his desk, writing orders, when one of Roosevelt's couriers pushed through the mosquito netting, saluted, and brought orders from the colonel.

"We need chow and ammunition bad, Captain," said the harried soldier. "We're getting low on everything, and the colonel says we're to make an infantry charge toward Spanish fortifications."

"Can you show me on the map?" said Plummer.

"Yes, sir," the courier said as he walked to the desk and looked intently at the detailed military map. Finally he touched his finger to the map. "They're right here, sir, near these co-ordinates."

"San Juan, Santiago," muttered Plummer. "Very well, we'll have the convoy on its way immediately. Now, did you run into any of the enemy on your way here?"

"No, sir, although I did see some movement across the open terrain to the south of the Hill."

Plummer dismissed the man, ordering him to get back to the American troops with the message that supplies were on the way. Within the hour, Plummer had assembled a few horses and mules to carry ammunition and, along with Horn and several troopers, was following a projected supply line toward the fray. The convoy moved quickly and as quietly as possible. The only sounds other than horses' and mules' hoofs plunking into the sandy loam were the constant slaps of the men to their necks and arms as they swatted at the ever-present mosquitoes.

Reaching an area of impenetrable vegetation and downed trees near the headwaters of a small stream, Plummer sent Horn ahead to scout a route around the deadfall. He loped off through the dense foliage a hundred yards to the east and found an opening. Wanting to scout the potential route before committing the convoy, he continued on a half mile, and was about ready to turn back and call the convoy forward when he noticed some disturbed ground ahead. Dismounting, he saw that three riders and four or five men on foot had passed through a small clearing, heading west. To his knowledge, there were no Americans in the area, so the men who made the tracks must be Spanish, and they were headed directly toward the American convoy.

Cursing quietly, Horn pulled his Winchester out of its scabbard, tied up his horse, and followed the tracks at a quiet lope. Minutes later, he crested a small hill and saw the men he trailed a hundred yards ahead, just beginning to fan out across a low ridge directly above Plummer and his men. The riders had dismounted, and one man seemed to be giving silent orders, gesturing to the others. They were Spanish soldiers, all right, and they were preparing to ambush the convoy.

Horn immediately scrambled off to the left, behind the cover of an earthen bank that seemed to be split by a massive tree with exposed roots. He quickly sighted his Winchester on the man in charge and squeezed off a round. He saw blood spurt from the man's back as he shot yet again, this time a little higher. The man's neck exploded. Horn had hated to take the extra instant to fire a second shot, but figured that once the leader was dead, chaos would set in.

Below, he saw the troopers of the American convoy take cover, not yet realizing their situation. Two Spanish soldiers attempted to turn around and return Horn's fire. He shot the first one in the head, causing his blood-spattered hat to fly several feet in the air. The second, he shot through the heart as he stood to run for cover. All but two of the others were exposed to Horn's sniping, and quickly threw down their weapons and raised their arms in surrender. Horn watched the remaining two men ensconce themselves in a rocky outcropping, effectively shielding themselves from fire.

In the stillness, Horn yelled: "Captain Plummer, I've cut off an ambush! They've surrendered, save fer two who holed up in the rocks right above you. Why don't you lob a mortar in there and roust them skunks?" Then speaking in Spanish, Horn repeated the phrase.

The two men immediately jumped up with their hands in the air, walked into the open, and sat down.

"Never mind, Captain!" he yelled as he reached up and flattened a mosquito that had been boring into his neck. "I think we got 'er handled."

Plummer and two troopers walked up the slope and collected the prisoners. Horn joined them to the grateful thanks of the Americans. After having the prisoners dig shallow graves for their dead companions, Plummer had their hands tied behind their backs and then ropes looped around their midsections, tying the ropes to packsaddles on two of the troop's mules.

As the group prepared to continue up the route Horn had scouted, Plummer pulled Horn aside and said: "Thank you, Tom. I believe we would have lost men if you hadn't spotted the ambush. Perhaps some of the old ways we learned in Arizona aren't outdated after all."

"Nope, Ed," Horn answered as he turned his horse forward once again to scout on ahead. "I guess they ain't. Maybe it's just war, though. Maybe that's all the Old West was. One big war."

Several hours later, the supply convoy reached Roosevelt's troops. The colonel greeted the convoy with his characteristic "Bully!" and immediately set history into motion. Freshly supplied and cocky as roosters in a hen house, the

Rough Riders saluted their comrades, put on their grim faces, and took off on foot to assault the Spanish fortifications on Kettle Hill, near San Juan. That day, a powerful American legend was born.

Below, Tom Horn could only marvel at the sight of the mounted Roosevelt, pistols drawn and reins clamped between his teeth, as he prepared to lead the charge. The man was either a military genius or a fool, Horn thought.

A few days later, Horn lay in a sweltering tent, delirious with fever. He'd begun feeling poorly after his return to the supply camp, and within no time was too weak to walk. The military doctor took one look at him and diagnosed the Cuban fever. He told Horn to hold on, because he'd likely get worse before he got better.

Plummer sat with Horn the first night through his delirium. He prepared a report to General Maus by lantern light, occasionally stopping to listen to Horn's ravings and ramblings. It was evident that somewhere inside, Horn was riding the vast expanse of the West, and that he felt he was being followed. He screamed in abject terror the names of men Plummer had never heard and talked in quickly accented Spanish. He warned Al Sieber of danger on several occasions, and feverishly repeated the names of some men named Bill Lewis and Fred Powell. He kept asking someone named Coble: "Why, John, why?"

Three days later, Horn was alert enough to know what was going on, but still weak as a pup. Plummer had learned that John Coble was Horn's friend and employer in Wyoming, and had wired Coble with the news that Horn had yellow fever and would be sent by train to Wyoming to recuperate.

As he escorted Horn to the transport that would take him back across the sea to Tampa, Plummer spoke of the ramblings he'd witnessed that first night. "Tom," he said, "you said some things when you were ranting and raving, some things that are hard to explain. Something's chasing you down, Tom. You were scared to death."

Horn merely looked at Plummer, then cast his eyes downward. "It's no never mind, Ed. It's just the fever. I'll get along, I 'spect."

"That you will, Tom," said Plummer. He mused for a moment, then added: "I knew from the first time I met you and Sieber that you were a man with two sides. I've known the right and proper man. I suppose your other self is not so noble. I've heard stories from some of the other men, you know. Stories of how you've become a gunman, almost a legend in the West. I don't doubt them, Tom. But if they're true, I hope you know when to quit, my friend."

Horn smiled weakly, and then chuckled. "Legend, you say? Hell, no, Ed. I'm just a guy who rides horses and stops rustlers. I drink a little too much on occasion, but that wind up in Wyomin' damn' near forces you into that condition." He chuckled again and continued: "No, I think you know all of me. We've done some fine things together, Ed. I'll see you on down the road, *mi amigo*." He gingerly climbed the side rail into the boat and was gone.

Now, looking into Glendolene Kimmell's eyes through the portal of a jail cell door, he wished he had met her earlier, that she had been waiting for him when he had shuffled off the train in Cheyenne and sat waiting for Coble's carriage. He wished that she had been with him through the night sweats and body-wracking nausea. He wished that she had taken care of him and nursed him back to health. Looking at her, he almost convinced himself that she had been, but he knew he hadn't met her until after the Brown's

Hole business. Until after the other side of his personality that Ed Plummer had recognized surfaced and killed again.

Here, in his freezing jail cell, he wanted to tell Glendolene Kimmell that he wished they had met sooner, under different circumstances. He supposed that's why he told her about Cuba during those afternoons under the endless Wyoming sky, and about the adventure he'd encountered there. He thought there would be an interest on her part, as if she had known him and lived vicariously through his eyes. As if she had been his wife. But he hadn't known her, and now as he shivered standing at the cell door, he could only respond to her questions, and to her eyes.

Reaching up to put a hand through the opening and lightly stroke the side of Horn's face, Glendolene Kimmell said: "How pale you've grown. As pale as the snow on the prairie."

Allowing her touch, Horn said: "Well, there's not much sunlight reaches into this cell, Myrt. I 'spect, if I get out, I'll get my color back."

She smiled sadly as she removed her hand and gripped one of the iron bars inserted through the small space. They engaged in small talk for a few minutes. She caught him up on the local gossip since her last visit the week before, and told him she had asked Clay Stephens to allow her a face-to-face visit in the next day or two. Before the scheduled hanging, anyway. She thought the lawman might allow it.

She said: "Tom, this town is a regular carnival, waiting for your murder! I despise these people. Every person out there knows you didn't shoot Willie Nickell. They know that your trial was a joke. They know that LeFors lied. Yet they don't have any courage, Tom. They can't bring themselves to allow you justice. Instead, they stand on street corners and talk about you. I overheard the butcher, Mister

Bates, say the most awful thing, and I wanted to hurt him, really hurt him. It's like that everywhere. They know you're innocent, but they're excited to have you die."

Horn raised his eyebrows in a quizzical look and said: "That so? What'd ol' butcher Bates have to say, anyhow?"

"Oh, nothing," she said as she shook her head from side to side. "It was just a bad joke. He apologized when he saw that I'd heard him."

They were quiet for a moment, then she said: "I have some hope, Tom. I don't know how or why, but I know that something is going on. John's been acting funny of late, comforting me, and that sort of thing. I think he believes you'll escape, somehow."

Horn merely looked at her. As hard as it was to resist her gaze, he knew he couldn't tell her about the plans for the hoax that Clay Stephens had dreamed up. He hoped that John Coble wouldn't let it slip, either. She was an observer, she had often said, and every observer he had ever known had talked as well. They couldn't wait to share their observations. And now his life depended on absolute secrecy.

"Myrt," he said, "I'm near about done with writin' down my story, my life's story, I guess. Clay lets me have writing materials now and again." He thought of the commotion caused by Clay Stephens's allowing him to have paper and pen in the first place, and how such privilege had been taken away for a time after he had smuggled out his allegations against the cattlemen. Now, the sheriff figured the damage was done, and was allowing Horn to set down his autobiography. "I'd like you to read it, to check for mistakes and such. Will you do that for me?"

She smiled back at him and said: "Absolutely, Tom. Anything you want."

"Thanks, Myrt. It *is* a pleasure to see your face."

They heard Clay Stephens, walking through his office, and knew the visit was nearing an end. Horn touched his face where her hand had been and said: "I'd like you to do somethin' for me, Myrt. I've got a little note here I wonder if you might deliver fer me. I'm in a letter writin' mood, I guess. Don't let Clay see it! He checks through everything I send out."

He slipped the folded note through the opening. She took it without looking and inserted it into a pocket of her coat.

Clay Stephens entered the cell corridor and cleared his throat, indicating that the visit was now over. Glendolene Kimmell kissed the tips of her fingers and reached through the opening, gently placing them on Horn's lips. She then turned and was escorted out by Stephens. In his office, she said that she would return in two or three days and once again requested a face-to-face meeting with Horn.

Stephens remained noncommittal and wished her a good day.

Outside, she walked down the frozen street for a block, then ducked into a general store. Inside, she handed a shopping list to the clerk, then sat near a well-stoked stove that heated the entire room. Reaching into her pocket, she took out the folded note Horn had slipped her and looked at the salutation. In Horn's scratchy handwriting, it read: **Personal for Mr. Hugh Carey**. She thought she remembered Hugh Carey as a cowboy on the Webster spread. In fact, she remembered meeting him at the very barn dance where she had watched a tall, raw-boned cowboy ride into the yard. She would deliver the note on her way back to Iron Mountain, she decided.

Hugh Carey, she thought. *What an interesting name.*

Chapter Twelve

He emerged from the dream to loud yelling and a continual banging on the cell door. Soaked with sweat, he opened his eyes wide and unconsciously put his fingers to his throat as if to slow down the raging blood pulsing through his veins. He felt as if his heart would burst and he was lost in the haze of senselessness. The pounding on the door continued as he tried to get his bearings. He sat bolt upright and stared uncomprehendingly at the door, slowly realizing that someone was yelling at him.

"Pipe down, Tom. God dammit! Yer havin' another 'n'. Another o' yer bad night dreams."

Clay Stephens's voice cut through the fog as Horn swung his legs off the cot. Looking dumbly at the door, he thought the pounding might never stop.

"Awright!" yelled Stephens. "Are you woke up now, Tom? Answer me, god dammit! It's three in the mornin', and you're stirrin' up half o' Wyomin' with yer god-damn' screamin'."

Horn wiped the sweat from his face with his hands, and then ran them across his trousers. "Yeah, Clay. I'm awake."

"Sit back on the bunk, then. I'm comin' in."

The sheriff opened the door and stuck in half his body. Satisfied that Horn was across the cell, he relaxed slightly and said: "I thought there was a murder goin' on in here. You were screamin' louder than you ever have, Tom."

Horn merely ran his fingers through his hair, then scratched his head.

"God knows you've got reason for nightmares," Stephens said gruffly, "but you don't have to worry about your sorry hide no more, Tom. You know the deal. You're gonna slip on outta here and off to Mexico in no time."

Horn said: "We need to talk, Clay. I need to know more about this deal."

"Later in the mornin'," said Stephens. "Stain and Coble's comin' in. We'll get the final plans all fixed up. Now you get yerself together and get back on to sleep." He looked sternly at Horn. "Quit dreamin' 'bout things you cain't change."

After the door had closed, Horn sat on the bunk without moving for nearly an hour. His head was spinning with the dream, with the strong-armed lawmen leading him through the town, with the crowd following, with Willie Nickell standing on the gallows, laughing.

It seemed as if he couldn't drift off any more without the dream showing up. The same dream every time—Willie standing at the top of the gallows stairs, holding the noose, and laughing his fool little head off.

God, he wished he could make Willie go away. But the boy haunted him in ways that Powell and Lewis could not. Sitting on the edge of the cot, he tried to figure out for the thousandth time how all this had happened, how he had turned into a man afraid to sleep for fear of a boy's ghost.

He supposed it began when he was bedridden at Coble's ranch, the Cuban fever running through him, turning his veins into rivers of fire, his muscles knotted in agonizing spasms. The fever was so bad he spent the better part of two weeks in and out of delirium, worried each time he came to that he had committed unspeakable slips of the tongue, that he had revealed secrets known only to him.

He had felt better when he arrived back in Wyoming. The fever had subsided somewhat, and he felt the dry air would do him good. John Coble had collected him from the carved maple bench at the station and helped him climb up onto the buckboard, his bag and rifle in tow. By the time they arrived at Coble's ranch, Horn thought he felt nearly cured. Coble convinced him to stay in a bedroom in the house for a few days, anyway, just in case. He was right. The next morning, the yellow fever came back with a vengeance, wracking his body with pain and unbelievable sweats. Over the next month, Horn rarely left the room, and often had to pull a cord attached to a bell to summon help.

By the time the fever had ebbed somewhat, Horn lay in bed day after day and thought of nothing but riding the range. He longed to sit on his stallion and ride for days or weeks, or even forever.

By the second month after his return, he was gaining both strength and weight, and had moved out into a bunkhouse. He sat for hours with Coble and discussed the events of Cuba, the older man listening intently, and occasionally asking questions. Slowly, over the days, they talked of other things as well. As they sat on a long bench against the wall of a sunny porch one afternoon after spending an hour or so in small talk, Coble had said: "You know, Tom, when you left the country for a while, word got around. Problems started up again. I know that Stain and some others want to talk to you about some detective work." Coble lowered his eyes, then continued. "I'll be straight with you. I'm stayin' as far away from this business as possible. I believe what we've done is right. I believe what we've asked *you* to do is right. But I'm tired of the killin', Tom. And I'm tired of what I see it doin' to you."

Horn sniffed quietly and leaned back on the bench and rubbed his back against the rough planking of the outer wall. Looking out across the open yard to the house, he said: "I'm a detective, John. I don't know what else to be. I was a scout once. I was a lawman once. I been a soldier and an interpreter and a cowboy and God knows what else. Now I'm a detective. That's just the way it is.

"Let me tell you somethin' I never told nobody else. You remember when the decision was made about them rustlers up to Horse Creek? I knew Powell, and I'd heard of Lewis. You know we tried everything we could to run them boys off, John. Everything. But in the end, it had to be done the hard way. I was willin' to do it. Mostly for the money, I admit, but I was willin'. So when it was done, I realized that it was just business.

"John, I ran to Cuba. I ran to Cuba like a scared dog because I couldn't stop seein' 'em."

"Seein' who?" asked Coble, puzzled.

"Lewis and Powell," Horn said forcefully. "I seen Lewis off ridin' the prairie, big as you please, years after he'd been laid underground. And I chased Powell down across the rails, but couldn't catch him. I knew he was dead, too, but I swear it was him just the same."

Coble looked at his friend and saw that a tic had appeared below his left eye, causing his cheek to twitch uncontrollably. He saw the strain on Horn's face, and decided to hear him out rather than interrupt.

"I know it sounds loco, John, but them boys was somehow after me. I never seen a ghost in my life, although I'd heard tell 'bout some hauntin's. All I know is what I seen. So, I ran off to Cuba. I know I told you I needed a break from cowboyin' and such, but I really ran off to escape Lewis and Powell. When I was there, John, I kilt three men I didn't know, three who were tryin' to ambush Ed Plummer and his convoy. When the killin' was goin' on, it took every bit of will to stop from shootin' the others, even though they'd throwed down their weapons. After that, I thought a lot about Lewis and Powell, and what it all meant. Then I got sick. But during that time, I realized that I couldn't run away from nothin'. I seen Powell and Lewis only because I *let* myself see 'em. Do you understand, John?"

Coble gave a nearly imperceptible nod and raised his hand slightly. "I don't know that I do, Tom," he answered softly.

"It's like this. I got a conscience like anybody else. But I never been bothered by taking a life that needed to be taken. I was worried when I had to stop myself from shootin' those men in Cuba, worried that I'd crossed some sort of line. But then I just knew somehow that was what Lewis and Powell wanted. They wanted me to have doubts, to be scared and confused.

"Since the day I beat the tar outta my Daddy and took off for the West, I ain't been scared of one thing, John. And I don't intend to be again. That's why I'm gonna keep on being a stock detective. If you and the others need me, and it sounds like you do, well, I'm still your man. I won't let some moldy ol' god-damn' ghosts stop me."

Horn stopped talking and looked directly at Coble. Embarrassed by his admission, he just shook his head and looked away.

"Like I said, I don't know that I understand everything, Tom," Coble said. "I just think it's likely become a little too easy for Stain and the others to ask you to do things they won't do themselves. I guess I'm one o' them boys, too, so I throw my ownself into the pot. You're a fine cowboy, Tom. Why don't you settle on a little piece o' land around here and do some ranchin'? It's hard work, but there sure as hell ain't no ghosts involved."

Horn laughed out loud as he looked at Coble. The two began laughing in unison at the absurdity of the situation. In the end, they both knew they couldn't see Horn behind a plow or herding livestock for months at a time.

"Naw, John," said Horn. "I'll just have to face my demons and spit 'em in the eyes. So, you say you don't know what Stain's got in mind?"

Coble shook his head and answered: "Nope. And I still don't wanna know, either. All I know is they asked me to talk to you, to see if you still wanna do range work." He paused shortly and pulled on his moustache. "Reckon I'll tell 'em yes."

Two weeks later, Horn met with Stain and several others, where he learned of the disappearance of large amounts of stock near the Colorado border. He was asked to investigate and take appropriate measures. He was also asked to use an alias if anyone asked who he was. It seemed that small ranchers and potential rustlers had heard much about Tom Horn and would be likely to blow him from the saddle should they actually run into him.

When he felt strong enough, he saddled up and traveled west and then south, across the Colorado border and down into Brown's Hole. He traveled what was becoming known as the Outlaw Trail. Always alone, he traveled quick and light, not wanting to run into any of the Hole in the Wall gang or any others who used the trail that extended from Wyoming down through Brown's Hole and over into Utah. He'd heard that Flat Nose George had been shot and killed a few months back over on the Green River in Utah. The last thing he needed now was to be hooked up with Kid Curry or Cassidy and some of them. His life wouldn't be worth a plug nickel then.

He allowed himself to feel nothing but an icy cool as he surreptitiously scouted the Brown's Hole territory and asked seemingly innocuous questions to ranch hands and the few merchants he ran across. Soon, he hired on as a cowboy, only to find that the leader of the outfit, Matthew Rash, was working a herd that didn't belong to him. To top it off, Rash was being rustled by a rustler, a one-eared ex-slave called Isom Dart.

It didn't take Horn long to scope out the situation. He made contact with Stain by sending a letter with a cowboy who was heading for Cheyenne for supplies. When the cowboy returned, he handed Horn a wrinkled letter sealed with wax. It had just two words: **Handle it**.

Two days later, Matt Rash walked into his cabin, only to find a note stuffed under the door telling him to get out of the country or die. Not a man to be pushed, he ranted and raved to the cowboys in his outfit that he would find and kill the man who dared to tell him to leave. He sat until late in the evening with one of the cowboys, a tall, raw-boned and mustachioed man who'd come down from Wyoming a few weeks earlier. He called himself Jim Hix. Although the man had a yellowish pall about him that was attributed to catching some tropical fever while in the Army, he was one of the best wranglers Dash had ever seen.

"God damn, Jim," Rash said, his features glowing red from the campfire in front of them, "I'll not be bullied outta my own place. I didn't leave Texas to come into this low-down, snake-infested country just to be run out. These big ranchers got to realize that, if they don't take care of their own stock, some of its gonna be picked up by other folks. It's always been that way. That don't make me or any of the others around here rustlers, 'cept'n maybe that one-eared black dog, Dart. If I pick up a few head now and again, it's nothin' that nobody don't do."

The cowboy merely nodded his head and allowed that it was tough to keep cattle out on the range straight, all right.

Several weeks later, Rash sat down for breakfast at the table in his cabin, and had just put a piece of bacon into his mouth when the first bullet shattered through the window, catching him in the upper chest. Before he could fall out of the line of fire, another ripped through his lower abdomen. Laying on the floor, he fought through the shock and realized that he was mortally wounded. The blood was fairly pumping from the wound below his heart, and he felt weaker by the second. Painfully rolling over on his side, he dipped his fingers into the pool of blood below, and attempted to write a message on the floor, a message saying that he'd been murdered by the big cattle interests to the north. As he began to make bloody marks on the floor, a scuffed boot stepped on his hand. He hadn't even heard the cabin door open, and was too weak to try to put up a fight. He went limp as the boot moved to his midsection and rolled him over on his back. As he felt himself fall into a deep mist, he looked up and wondered what Jim Hix was doing there. *Funny,* he thought, *he should be out on the range.*

The killing of Rash caused considerable concern in Brown's Hole, with each of the small ranchers arming themselves and staying alert for danger. Jim Hix disappeared after a while, and no one thought much about it. Meanwhile, the rustling continued.

Isom Dart was a thief. He felt it to be an honorable profession and had done quite well at it over the years. He'd been in a few scrapes, all right, but had managed to pull through with only a scar or two. Except for the ear, of course. He told everyone that an Indian tomahawk had chopped it off when a brave found him bunked up with a willing squaw. Actually he'd been stealing chickens from a poor farmer in Mexico in the middle of the night. As he ran with a fowl under each arm, the farmer had stepped in front of him with a raised axe and swung down. Diving in time to save his life, Dart, nonetheless, had lost his ear, as well as the chickens.

The pain and indignity of having one ear chopped off notwithstanding, Dart continued his career of petty crime, becoming an accomplished horse thief and, by the time he wandered into Colorado, a cattle thief as well.

A man who had generally escaped danger, Dart figured that anyone who had lived as long as he had after being born a slave could brag about beating the odds anyway.

Dart and several others had holed up in a small cabin while putting together a herd made up of cattle from various places, mostly strays belonging to other outfits. They figured on fattening the cattle before driving them over to Utah for sale.

Dart awoke early, stood from his cot, and stretched. He walked to the cabin's only window and peered out at the first rays of dawn, just emerging over the eastern hills. It looked like a dreadful day, with high winds and a storm brewing. He whooped and hollered, rousting the three other men in the cabin, before opening the door to step out and relieve himself. The bullet hit him directly between the eyes, exiting the back of his head on its way to being lodged in the back wall, splattering blood and brains over the three men arising behind him. The one-eared thief stood for a moment, swaying in the doorway, before falling forward in a heap. One of the men shoved the door shut and slid to cover behind the cabin's thick log walls. The others followed suit. They would stay there until nightfall.

Two hundred yards to the east, behind a close grouping of pine trees, Jim Hix backed away from cover and slid his Winchester .30-30 into its scabbard. He walked to his horse, mounted, and headed off to the north, to Wyoming.

Horn remembered the long ride back to Cheyenne, and the meeting with Stain that had left him $1,000 richer. "Well, Mister Hix," Stain had said, "you did a fine job."

Chapter Thirteen

Horn began to drink heavily after the Brown's Hole business. He became a regular at several saloons, gaming establishments, and bordellos along the North Platte River. Once, when he was nearly immobilized from bad whisky at a whorehouse in Rawlins, he thought he saw a one-eared black man, but he passed out before he could be sure. Another time, he drew a pistol on someone he thought had called him Hix. The burly saloonkeeper sneaked up from behind and grabbed his arms before he could shoot the bewildered man.

He drifted and worked for several outfits over the next couple of years, yet was always at the ready should the cattle interests require his services as a stock detective. Stain and his group were quiet, not using Horn, but retaining him as part of a deal made before the Brown's Hole killings. In quiet times, they made sure he had work as a cowboy when it was needed.

Horn had thought he would have to kill Kels Nickell when John Coble was stabbed. He was on his way when Coble had grabbed his hand as he sat by the cattleman's bed. Coble had looked up with a terrible demeanor and shook his head as forcefully as he could. "No. When the time is right," he had said in a whisper.

Horn had met and wooed Glendolene Kimmel for the past couple of months, and had felt himself become more and more lost. He was at first flattered by her attentions, and took full advantage of such flattery. But as their relationship evolved, he began to feel like a trophy of some sort, or a specimen in a museum. Each time she observed that he was one of the last of the frontiersmen, he felt more and more like the tiger pacing in its St. Louis cage. He tried honestly to assess his feelings toward her, but found that he had few feelings left. Most had disappeared from sight over the years and were as elusive as Geronimo's band of Chiricahuas. Although he enjoyed her company and was at times captivated, he still held back, choosing to find fault with her in any number of small ways.

He had it out with her, letting her know that he was just a man, no better or worse than many. He wasn't some sort of god-damned cowboy idol, he said. She looked at him with her infinitely deep eyes and said she understood, that she had been wrong to form conclusions about him based on her own preconceptions. Yet, he thought that deep down she still looked at him as a scientist does a bug, with keen interest and little else. He told her he'd drop by as soon as he figured out what was going on in his head. She quietly assented.

And so it was when John Stain had contacted Horn early in the summer of 1901, proposing a meeting between Horn and ex-Governor Ford. A meeting about Kels Nickell.

Horn had walked away from the meeting feeling as dirty and disgusted as William Ford had acted when they shook hands. Despite all the fawning and expressions of gratitude, he knew that everyone but Coble looked at him as what he was, a hired killer. When he left the governor's office in the pouring rain and walked across the street to the hotel to enter a drunken card game, he looked back and saw Stain, standing in the window. It was all he could do not to fetch his Winchester and shoot the man down. After pausing, he merely raised his hand and waved, instead.

Horn stayed in the card game for nearly two days without sleep before mounting his horse and heading back out to John Coble's place. He slept for twenty hours straight before riding south all the way to Greeley, Colorado. There, he took a room and drank for the next three days, now and again frequenting a gambling hall south of town. He mused on and off about Kels Nickell. He'd met the man often enough and knew of his infamous temper, but had never had trouble with him. In fact, he'd seen Nickell riding a bay mare along his fence line on numerous occasions.

He hadn't really decided to kill Nickell, not until he was tucked away in a sweltering room in Greeley. But the more he thought of Nickell's treatment of Coble, the more he knew that for the first time in his life, killing would be easy. John Coble was the only man other than Al Sieber who had known Horn for a long period of time and still called him friend. Coble often saw things in Horn that were invisible to anyone else, and even to himself on occasion. The fact that an extra $500 was thrown in was meaningless. He found that it was easy to hate Kels Nickell. The man had hurt his friend.

Horn returned to Coble's spread, only to find a messenger from Stain with money in hand. He took the $500 and stashed it in his waistcoat pocket. The next day, after allowing his horse to rest from the long journey of the past week, he saddled up and took off at a leisurely pace, telling the other cowhands that he was off to check for strays and signs of rustlers. He headed directly for Iron Mountain.

He camped that night on a rocky outcropping above a small creek that bubbled up out of the ground a few miles to the north. It was a dry camp, with no fire. He left his horse saddled, disengaging the scabbard and rifle and carrying them under his arm as he hiked a few yards up into the rocks. He pushed his way into a hollow between two boulders and spent the night looking at the stars as they passed across the cloudless sky. Sometime after midnight, clouds started coming in, riding the west wind. He watched them slowly cover the sky, shading the moon and obscuring its light. He stared straight ahead after that, his mind unalterably on the task he would undertake in the morning.

As dawn approached, he noted with curiosity that ground fog began to appear below his perch, the result of the cooling weather coming into contact with warm earth. He stood and stretched and pounded his thighs with his fists to limber himself up. He retrieved the scabbarded rifle from where he'd leaned it against a boulder and walked down from the rocks a few yards to his horse, leading it by the reins for a couple of hundred yards before mounting.

In the darkness, Horn moved like a spirit across the fog-shrouded prairie. The *clip-clop* of his horse's hoofs was muffled by the fog, making a dull and foreboding sound. Like an avenging angel, he seemed to glide through the mist, intent on his mission of death and destruction.

Shortly before dawn, he tied his horse to a willow by the bank of a tiny, crystal-clear stream. He removed his boots and stockings, stashing them behind a willow. He wanted to leave no telltale scuffs in the landscape for experienced trackers to follow and knew that bare feet left little or no sign. He grabbed his Winchester and stepped into the stream, walking against the stream's weak current for nearly a quarter mile before emerging onto a rocky patch, his feet nearly frozen. He rubbed them with his woolen neckerchief until they were dry and had some feeling. Then he began walking toward the home of Kels Nickell.

In the fog, he relied on both instinct and previous knowledge of the area to guide him to his destination. He continued walking, stepping on stones when possible, until he crested a fog-shrouded ridge. There, he lay down on a patch of granite rubble a half mile from the Nickell spread. He intended on waiting for the fog to abate before quietly sneaking closer, perhaps even into the corral area where Nickell kept his sheep.

He lay on the rocks for the better part of an hour, peering intently for any sign of movement in the slowly disappearing fog. He was shivering uncontrollably and felt like his whole body had gone numb from cold and lack of comfort, but knew that diligence was a price that always had to be paid. The bleating of Nickell's sheep reached him through the fog, and he thought that they might be getting nearer. He heard a horse neigh just as the fog began to lift.

Within minutes, he had a hazy view of the rocky slope before him. There, nearly three hundred yards away and through the patchy fog, sat Nickell on the gray mare he always rode into Cheyenne. His brown flat-brimmed hat jammed firmly on his head, he was herding some sheep through a gate, taking them out to a pasture that wasn't his. Horn raised the rifle, took a deep breath to control his quaking, and sighted the gun at the figure's back below. He grimly noted that this would be the last time the man would use someone else's property to feed his sheep.

Horn placed the first bullet directly between Nickell's shoulder blades, and followed it an instant later with another for good measure. Through the patchy fog, he saw Nickell pitch forward and try to grasp the horse's neck. The mare reared at the same time and took off through the fog.

Horn couldn't see where Nickell had landed, or if his

shots had killed him. Quietly cursing, he stood, picked up and pocketed the two shell casings on the ground, then carefully picked his way down the slope, stopping every few yards to make sure that he heard nothing but the bleating of sheep. As he approached the gate, he saw Nickell lying on the ground near a patch of yucca. He had crept about twenty yards toward his home, leaving a trail of blood behind him, smeared into the dirt by his legs as he crawled. He was on his stomach with his hands below him. Horn quickly stepped up to the body and jabbed it with his rifle barrel. There was no movement. Taking care to be quiet, he reached down and grabbed Nickell's shoulder in order to turn him over. He was surprised at how light the man was. Nickell had been a large man, in Horn's estimation.

He quickly flipped the body over and, for the first time in his life, nearly screamed from shock and fear. The face of a boy stared up at him, his blue eyes open, his peach-fuzzed face locked in a grimace of anguish. The face glowered at Horn, the dead eyes accusing him and damning him straight to hell in a single instant.

Stifling a cry, Horn frantically threw his rifle down and ripped open the boy's bloody shirt to see if the wounds were fatal. All he saw was a gory hole the size of his fist where both bullets had exited, taking most of the boy's heart with them. That he'd managed to crawl at all was astonishing.

In shock, Horn wavered over the boy, all the while making guttural sounds while picking up the brown hat and then throwing it down again. His quivering was not from the cold now. Rather it was from the absolute trauma of the occurrence. He'd killed a boy, for God's sake. A boy he didn't even know. *He must be one of Nickell's brood,* he thought. *But how could I have shot him? He's just a boy!*

Thinking of nothing else he could do, he gently raised

the boy's head and moved a smooth flat stone underneath. Gingerly resting the head on the rock, Horn reached down and closed the boy's eyes.

"I'm sorry," he muttered. "I'm so sorry, boy. It's all a mistake. You can't be dead, can you? Why were you wearin' your pa's hat, ridin' his horse? I . . . I don't know how this happened."

Dumbly realizing that someone might have heard the shots, Horn stood, grabbed the rifle, and ran up the slope as fast as he could. As he ran, he reached into his pocket, grabbed the shell casings, and threw them into a group of boulders near the gate. By the time he reached the outcropping where he had fired the fatal bullets, his feet were bloody and torn from rocks, cacti, and yucca, but he didn't feel anything except overwhelming fear and revulsion at what he'd done. He kept running, because running was the only thing he could do.

Splashing into the chilly stream, Horn tried to calm himself down by cupping water and throwing it on his face. The shock helped bring his mind back to physical matters, but he couldn't shake the enormity of the crime he'd committed. Slowly now he picked his way down the stream, emerging at the spot where his horse was tied. He forced himself to sit down and remove the most aggravating of the cactus spines before painfully yanking on his stockings and boots.

His mind was slowly starting to function once again, so he compelled himself to ride steadily, and to think. He began shivering again, this time from both the morning chill and the enormity of his actions. He rode south, and cut cross-country to Coble's spread. He made sure that no one was around, then grabbed some clothes and scribbled a quick note for Coble, saying he needed a few days to himself. He then took off again, this time for Denver.

He remembered very little of the two months he spent in Denver. He immediately headed for a hotel on Market Street, where he spent four days in a room with little but whisky and tequila. When he emerged, the *Rocky Mountain News* that was in the hotel lobby carried a story about a boy being killed from ambush north of Cheyenne. Willie Nickell, his name was. Horn sighed and stared at the paper for nearly an hour.

The only way he could stand to be awake was by being drunk, so he drank. He realized he would soon kill himself, but he kept on. In the end, self-preservation took hold, and he slept for nearly two days and awoke ravenously hungry. He reserved a bath and cleaned up, noticing for the first time as he combed his hair in a beveled mirror how much he resembled his father. He resisted the impulse to shatter the mirror, instead walking out for his first real meal in nearly a week.

Two weeks later, he retrieved his horse from the hotel's livery stable and rode down Bannock Street for a couple of miles in search of a saloon he used to frequent. In a field near the railroad tracks stood a two-story brick building with a dilapidated hitching post. Three horses were tethered to the post, and a shabby black buggy was stopped outside, its team tied to a scrawny elm tree. A sign over the entrance read BUCKHORN EXCHANGE. He knew Bill Cody had spent considerable time there, drinking and playing cards. He understood it held a poolroom now, and thought he might spend a few hours there.

Inside, he started drinking beer served in large steins. He looked at himself in the back-bar mirror and thought that he'd been haunted, indeed. He had lost considerable weight and had black circles around his eyes. He made himself stop thinking about the causes of his dreadful appearance by switching to whisky, and then pouring whisky into beer.

Several hours later, he found himself in conversation with a railroad man who had come in following his twelve-hour shift of replacing rails near the saloon. A bulky, black-bearded man with arms like oaks, he downed three or four beers as he talked with the drunken cowboy at the bar. When Horn got around to calling the railroad man's mother a soiled dove from the bowels of Dublin, the man hit him so hard that he skidded across the dingy hardwood floor and landed unconscious, with his head resting against a spittoon.

When he awoke, he found that his head was encased in plaster of Paris. He moaned loudly, and a nun came into his vision. "Well, Mister Horn," she said, "you join the living. I'm Sister Theresa, and you're at Saint Luke's Hospital. You've had a broken jaw, so you'll be with us for a while, I'm afraid. The police doctor patched you up, but you'll be staying here."

Horn moaned softly.

"You should be glad that the colonel who runs the Buckhorn is honorable," Sister Theresa continued. "You had over three hundred and fifty dollars which he turned over to us. And your horse is stabled at his home."

She smiled and winked as she said: "It's nice to have a paying patient, Mister Horn."

Chapter Fourteen

Three weeks later, Horn once again mounted his horse and took off for Wyoming. Once he was back at Coble's ranch, he learned that all hell had broken loose over the Nickell boy's murder. In fact, Horn's name had come up. Then Kels Nickell had been shot three times, but he was too mean to die in most people's assessment. Coble suggested that Horn should immediately contact those conducting the inquest in order to explain his whereabouts. He did just that, and told them he had been at the Coble Ranch as well as out scouting for strays to the south, far away from the gate at Iron Mountain where Willie Nickell had met his death.

By then, without his knowledge, Clay Stephens had brought in Joe LeFors. Also a stock detective by trade, LeFors claimed to walk a straight line when it came to the law. In fact, he never walked on the line, he stepped over it. LeFors had told the cattlemen as well as Clay Stephens of his suspicion that Horn had shot the boy, but there was nothing in the way of concrete proof.

John Stain's relief at the lack of evidence was tempered by the guilt he felt at having sent Horn on his mission. He met secretly with John Coble, telling him that he understood that Horn might be involved. Coble disbelieved him, but agreed to talk to Horn about his silence should there be an arrest. In the meantime, Clay Stephens had convinced

Stain and Ford that someone had to be accountable. If Horn had done it, so be it. If not, he was still a dangerous man who should be put away.

The trap was sprung when LeFors sent a wire to Horn with the offer of a job in Montana. The job dealt with "secret work" that needed to be done to protect the cattle industry. Out of money, Horn eagerly replied, and the two decided to meet in Cheyenne. Horn was in his cups by the time LeFors met him at the train station. The two went to a saloon and had a few drinks, and then walked across the street to continue their conversation in the empty U.S. marshal's office.

Horn felt as if he'd been drunk for years and knew the last thing he should be doing was getting friendly with a stock detective who was now wearing a marshal's badge. But since the shooting, he hadn't cared about much except alcohol. He had met LeFors on numerous occasions ranging clear back to the invasion of Johnson County. He knew him to be a peer, a man in the same business. Badge or no badge, he thought he could be open, maybe even joke a little.

The two sat on hard straight-backed chairs while LeFors talked about the job in Montana.

"Tom, they're good people," he said. "I've worked for 'em for five or six years. You'll have to get right in among 'em and gain their confidence. Show 'em you're all right."

Horn shook his head and put up his hands. "I don't want to be making reports to anybody at any time. I'll simply have one report to make, and that'll be my final report." His eyes were bleary, and his speech was slightly slurred. "If a man has to make reports all the time, they will catch the wisest son-of-a-bitch on earth." Suddenly he sat erect and pointed his finger at LeFors. "These people ain't afraid of shootin', are they?"

"No," answered LeFors, "they are not afraid of shooting."

"I shoot too much, I know," Horn slurred, his head bobbing and his right hand stabbing the air to accent his words. "You know me when it comes to shootin'. I'll protect the people I'm workin' for, but I've never got my employers into any trouble, yet, over anythin' I've done. A man can't be too careful because you don't want any god-damn' officers to know what you're doing."

LeFors chuckled in agreement. Then, offhandedly, he said: "Tom, I know you're a good man for the place. You're the best man to cover up your trail I ever saw. In the Willie Nickell killing, I could never find your trail, and I pride myself on being a trailer."

Horn stared at LeFors and absorbed the compliment. Suddenly, and without thinking, he was talking. "No, god damn. I left no trail. The only way to cover up your trail is to go barefooted."

Surprised, LeFors's eyebrows nearly formed a peak above his nose. "Where was your horse?" he asked.

"A god-damn' long ways off."

Horn remembered little of what was said after that. He did remember LeFors asking him about his weapon, though.

"What kind've gun have you got?" he said.

"I use a Thirty-Thirty Winchester," said Horn.

"You think that'll hold up as good as a Thirty-Forty?" LeFors said as he rubbed his chin.

"No," answered Horn, "but I like to get close to my man. The closer the better."

LeFors swallowed hard and asked: "So how far was Willie Nickell killed?"

Horn's head was drooping, and he shook it back and forth. "About three hundred yards," he said dumbly. "It was the best shot that I ever made and the dirtiest trick I ever done."

Of course, they came and arrested him after that. When he was sobered up, he realized he should have known that LeFors was after something, and that hidden witnesses were present. But he also knew he was beyond caring.

He told Coble that he had nothing to do with the kid's murder, that LeFors's so-called confession was just a bunch of lies and mixed-up transcriptions. When Glendolene Kimmell visited the jail, he told her the same thing. He told everyone the same thing.

The trial was a joke, an absolute mockery. There was no evidence other than the drunken confession that no one believed, coerced by a man no one respected. Yet, Sheriff Clay Stephens knew how to read the public, and he knew the only salve that would serve to heal the wound opened by a young boy's murder would be to hang somebody. Horn was as good as any.

After he was convicted, he managed a half-hearted jail-break by tricking a dimwitted deputy, only to be beaten to pulp by the angry citizens of Cheyenne who followed him into a wheat field. His most vivid recollection, while being pummeled, was of a sheepman's hat flying from his head and being carried over the field by an immense gust of wind.

John Coble came to visit religiously, and secured a promise of silence from Horn. He was so numb inside that he figured adherence to some code of honor might make him feel something, anything. It didn't.

It was then that the dreams began, that Willie Nickell

began visiting him each time he nodded off. At first, he was petrified. Then, he began displaying some annoyance. Whether it was out of boredom or lack of alcohol or both, for some strange reason he began writing down the pertinent facts of his life. He began to have emotions again, even if they were fear and self-loathing. After weeks of thought, he figured that his death would prove nothing, but that his life might hold something.

One afternoon, he asked Stephens for pen and paper and began writing a piece of correspondence. Beads of sweat stood out on his forehead as he began writing on the page.

The Honorable Federal Prosecutor
Denver, Colorado

Dear Sir:

My name is Tom Horn, and I have served in the employ of the Wyoming Stockmen's Association off and on for the past ten years. During that time, I have undertaken the control of rustlers and sheepmen within the state of Wyoming and without. At the behest of members of this organization, I have intimidated and scared off dozens of rustlers. Others, I have shot and killed. Each of these killings was done on the direct orders of a group of cattlemen who paid me to undertake such actions. Their names are as follows: Ex-Governor William Ford, Mr. John Stain, Mr. Peter Cooper. . . .

By the time he finished, Horn had named each of the stockmen he had worked for, including the dates he had performed stock detective work. He outlined each of the murders he had performed for the cattle interests, and also identified other unsolved murders he attributed to them. He admitted reluctantly to the killing of Willie Nickell. He had to stop momentarily to let three drops of sweat that had dripped on the page dry. When he continued, he calmly and clearly outlined the complicity of William Ford and John Stain in the murder. When he was finished, he had four pages implicating the most influential men in Wyoming in the murders of nearly a dozen men. And a boy.

When he signed the missive, he felt something like a flood of relief well up through him. He had set the record straight, as best as he knew how. At least if they hanged him, the document would find its way to the law, and he figured the cattle interests would, at the very least, be ruined, if not jailed and hanged themselves.

He inserted the letter in an envelope Stephens had given him, and sealed it. He left it unaddressed.

The next day his range partner, Hugh Carey, visited. Clay Stephens knew and liked Carey, so he allowed a private visit, although Carey had to stand outside the cell door and peek in at the prisoner.

"Hugh, it's good to see you," said Horn. "It's been a while."

"Yep, that it has," said the cowboy. He was stick thin with a lined face from years of prairie sun and wind, and Horn had gained his trust over the years. He was known throughout the border country of Colorado and Wyoming for his elaborately tooled belt, a thick strip of top-grained leather with a group of Indians chasing a lone cowboy engraved along its length.

They had talked for nearly a half hour about news and gossip when Horn walked to his bunk and picked up a letter. He came back to the door and grasped one of the bars bisecting the opening. He was quiet for a moment, thinking of how best to approach Carey, and then said: "Hugh, I'd like to ask for a powerful favor."

"Sure, Tom," Carey answered in a puzzled tone of voice.

"If I hang, I would like you to make sure this letter reaches the federal prosecutor in Denver. What's in this letter will likely save my life just by you holdin' it, but, if it don't, I hope I can count on you to deliver it."

He lifted the letter to the opening and watched as Carey gingerly took it.

"Um, Tom. I don't know," he said. "What's this about?"

"I can't tell you, Hugh. It's somethin' you'd be best not knowin', anyhow. Right now, it's just a way to save my life."

Carey stood silent for a moment, looking down at the letter he held between his hands. At length, he looked Horn directly in the eyes and said: "Tom, I have to know. Did you do it? Did you kill that boy?"

Horn reaffirmed his grip on the bar and said: "Hugh, as God is my witness, I did not."

Carey sighed and said: "Sure, Tom. I'll make sure your letter gets to Denver when they hang you."

Horn nodded in appreciation. The irony that Carey held the refutation to Horn's denial in his hands was something that he had to live with, he supposed.

Later, when Carey had gone, Horn lay down on his cot and began looking at the pattern of rivers on the ceiling. Soon he had nodded off.

He wasn't sure where he was. The town looked familiar, and he thought it might be in Wyoming, but everything seemed wrong. He couldn't identify any buildings, or any people for that matter. . . .

It had been that way ever since.

Chapter Fifteen

Glendolene Kimmell sat in the double-seated buggy and bundled up. The ride back to the ranch would be long, and she was in a hurry after taking the time to track down Hugh Carey. Now, she impatiently turned and looked for Jim Miller to appear so the rancher could take her back to her tiny room, so she could be warm and read her books.

She despised Miller, but figured that she might be able to talk him into telling her who had shot Willie and Kels Nickell. She was sure it was he, and thought she could surely aid Tom Horn by gaining a confession.

Earlier she had run into Frank Webster on the street and inquired as to Hugh Carey's whereabouts. The cattleman told her that the cowboy was in town having two troublesome horses shod at the livery, and asked if there was anything he could do. She had declined politely and excused herself, walking toward the stable several blocks away. She hadn't noticed Clay Stephens walk up to Webster and two of his cowhands, nor had she noticed them watch her move on down the street.

She couldn't quite keep from opening and reading the note Horn had given her when she had been basking in the warmth of the stove in the general store. Its message was intriguing and, to her, absolutely baffling.

Dear Friend Hugh:

Please forget our previous agreement. If I am hanged, as is most likely, please hold onto the correspondence we exchanged for three months before delivering it. I have reasons.

Tom

She thought about the message as she walked to deliver it, and tried to decipher its meaning. When she reached the stable and entered, she hoped to engage Carey in conversation, and perhaps find out what secret he held. But the cowboy was brusque, thanking her and stuffing the note into his pocket without even reading it. He excused himself and returned to his horses, leaving her standing alone.

She quickly returned to the general store, where she secured her supplies and left. Jim Miller was to meet her shortly to drive her back to Iron Mountain. Had she been in less of a hurry to pull secrets from him, she would have seen Webster and his men enter the livery.

Tom Horn sat in the same chair in Clay Stephens's office that he had several days earlier when he laid out his ultimatum to John Stain. Shackled as before, he watched the light snow fall from the gray sky as he waited. Stephens sat across the room, staring into space, seemingly unconcerned about the prisoner at the table.

Horn turned his head toward Stephens and said: "You look a mite peaked, Clay. Looks like you could use a little sleep."

A no-nonsense man of little humor, Stephens merely snorted and continued looking away. Just when Horn thought the sheriff had forgotten the remark, he said: "This dreamin' of yours is gettin' outta hand, Tom. You need to live a cleaner life."

"I'm plannin' on it," Horn replied. "I'll live one hell of a clean life in Mexico. Might even send you up a bottle o' mescal or two."

Stephens shook his head in annoyance and said: "Now there you go again, Tom, fergettin' that none of us are ever gonna have contact with you again in this life. Onct you're outta here and south o' the border, you'd best stay that way, or these boys'll likely set a stock detective or two on your trail."

The thought of a double-cross had constantly been on Horn's mind, but he'd played all of his cards. Now all he could do was make himself think about a fast horse and the Río Grande.

"Clay, how'd you get wrapped up with this outfit, anyway. You seem to be a law-abidin', God-fearin' man. Hell, if some fancy lawyer finds you out, they'd swing you from a higher tree than me."

Stephens turned a wary eye toward Horn and answered in a low tone. "There ain't nothin' wrong with protectin' a man's property. I'll admit, sometimes these boys have crossed the line, but it's been without my knowledge. I run a clean town here. Livestock rustlers ain't welcome. If they were, my town wouldn't be so clean now, would it?"

For what seemed the first time in months, Horn smiled and slowly began laughing. "So you're tellin' me I been doin' your job for you? Is that it, Clay?"

Stephens merely stared at Horn and said: "By God, I've done my best to reconcile this situation with your best interests in mind, Tom. I come up with a plan, and I sold them boys on it. When you ride out on the prairie south o' here next week, free as a bird, it'll be because of me. Because I saw no sense in killin' someone who's done their dirty work all these years."

Horn sneered and said: "Right. And I suppose my message to the federal prosecutor had nothin' to do with it. Hell, for all you know, Clay, your name could be right in there, right next to Ford's."

"Yeah, and for all you know them cattle boys'll find your little message before hangin' time." He stared ominously at Horn and said: "Don't think they ain't lookin'."

Horn was about to respond when two figures passed by the window and John Stain and John Coble stepped through the door. Horn thought he had never seen two such opposite men in the same room. Stain, dressed in his predictable black suit and black hat, provided a counterpoint to Coble's casual denim clothes and light gray Stetson. Stain's pinched, serious face contrasted with Coble's open, friendly features. And, of course, each man responded to Horn in his own way.

"Howdy, Tom," John Coble said in his soft drawl.

Horn smiled and nodded as the men removed their jackets and sat at the table.

"We'd best get started," Coble said. "We wanna make sure this goes off without a hitch. Now, Clay, tell Tom here how you got this set up."

Stephens walked over and joined the men. "I haven't told Tom a durn' thing about this, boys, so now's the time. It's mighty simple. I'll make sure the gallows are draped . . . an' draped high. In fact, I've got two men workin' on it right now, building four-foot rails around the platform, which is already six, seven feet off the ground. That means we'll have eleven, twelve foot o' drape. Down below, outta sight, we'll have a wagon waitin'.' The witnesses'll be able to see me 'n' Tom walk up the stairs. They'll see me reach over and shuck a noose around his neck before we walk behind the drape. They'll still see Tom's head and shoulders with the rope around his neck about ready to take him off to eternity. Now, this's where it'll be a little tricky. I've done this a hunderd times over the past week, Tom, so's I know it'll work.

"The noose'll be for show, only. Actually, it'll be one great big slipknot, and, the minute you fall, it'll slide from around your neck. I've even got a stiff collar made for you to wear to make sure you don't get no rope burn. The rope tyin' your hands behind your back'll be a slipknot, too. And you can slip out of it once you're behind the curtain, so long as you keep your hands around your back so's your shoulders don't come forward and look peculiar for a man about to be hanged."

Horn looked at Stephens incredulously, and started to speak.

"No, no, Tom. Now hear me out before you start screechin'. By that time, you'll be below anybody's line of sight 'cept me and Pete Cooper and one o' my deputies, who'll be standin' on the platform with me. They won't know that I'll have attached a clasp to a harness ring on the back o' the noose. Now, the clasp is hooked to another short rope that leads to some sacks o' flour that'll be placed on the trap door with you. When I spring the trap door, both you and the flour sack'll be steppin' into mid-air. The only difference is, your slipknot is gonna give way, and you'll land in a wagon bed below. Don't worry, it'll be filled with straw. The flour sacks'll be hangin' there, though, pulling that rope tight as can be. Every man there will think you've been hanged."

It was the most talking Horn had ever known Stephens to do. He sat and listened to the plan, shook his head, and said: "Hell, no. That's the worst plan I ever heard tell of. There's a hunderd ways things can go wrong."

"Like how?" challenged Stephens.

"Like the bags don't hold. Or they bump into me and cause me to fall into the side of the platform, break my neck or somethin'. Or the platform don't hold all that weight. Hell, I don't know. It just doesn't seem like somethin' a grown-up man would think up, that's all. Why don't you just close off the hangin' and tell everybody it's a private affair? Then, you just don't hang me and tell everyone you did."

He looked hopefully at the three men and raised his shackled hands for a response. Stephens was miffed, his face glowing bright red.

"That won't work," said Stain. "Like it or not, Tom, this affair has become a circus. Everyone in Wyoming will say they were there, whether they were or not. No, they have to see you hang, or believe they did. We even have Doc Pride ready to tell the crowd that you expired and that your body will be shipped to your brother down in Colorado. Hell, we even have a body, some fella that looks kinda like you. Sheepherder I guess, to put in your coffin. You haven't seen your brother in several years. If he decides to look at the body, I don't think he'll question the identity."

"It still won't work," said Horn with a raised voice. "They ain't gonna believe all this shill work. Now, if you was to have me wear some sorta brace or somethin', that might work."

"Tom," said John Coble in a soft voice, "I b'lieve it's a mite too late to go changin' plans. I thought you might have problems with this, so I checked it out." Coble smiled and opened his collar, showing Horn a thin red stripe on the right side of his neck. "I let 'em hang me this mornin' . . . to see if it all works."

Horn was flabbergasted, his eyes wide. "You're kiddin'!" he exploded. "John, how could you do that? You could 'a' been killed!"

Coble shook his head and gave Horn a self-effacing grin. "I had problems with Clay's plan, too," he continued. "So's I decided to put it to the test. I got me a little neck burn, here, when the knot slipped, but other than that I landed on a pile o' hay in the back of a wagon, all in one piece. It was kind of a thrill, really. The only problem was the collar," he said, rubbing his neck. "Clay needs to make sure it's put a little higher on you."

Horn was speechless. He looked from man to man, opening his mouth and shutting it again without saying a word. Finally he said: "What then?"

Stephens looked at the two cattlemen, and then continued: "You'll cover yourself up with straw. In the meantime, we'll make a show of takin' your body down, below the drape, where nobody can see. We'll lower the flour bags to you, and you can cover them up, too. I'll have another noose ready to show folks . . . say it was the one that hanged Tom Horn. Then, we'll slide your coffin onto the back o' the wagon, mebbe even give a few people a far away peek of a body in the coffin, wearin' clothes like yours. Then, we'll take the wagon on to the train station and load the body. Three deputies'll be there to guard it, makin' sure no one gets nosy. Meantime, we take the wagon out towards John Coble here's place. Your horse'll be packed and waitin'." He looked sternly at Stain. "Your money'll be waitin', too, right, John?"

"Absolutely," answered Stain.

"You say you have a body now?" asked Horn. "It'll be a little ripe by next week, won't it?"

"Webster's got it out at his ice house," said Stephens.

"Froze solid as a board. We'll let it thaw out come Thursday."

Horn merely sat at the table, his shoulders slumped. Everything had happened so quickly. He had written the memorandum to the federal prosecutor, then the note to Governor Ford. The next thing he knew, everything was moving at double speed. He hadn't taken the time to think about how Stephens's plan would actually be implemented. He just figured they'd come up with some sort of plan. But now that he heard it, he realized that it was a little less than half-baked. He said: "I don't like it. I don't like it one bit. But Stain, you and Stephens here better realize that, if you double-cross me, if for some reason that rope doesn't slip, you'll be swingin' from a proper gallows down in Denver in no time."

Stain shot Horn a venomous stare and said: "This'll work. I know it sounds too impossible to believe, but I watched John here fall down into the wagon bed with no problems. It worked slicker than goose shit, Tom. Now, if you don't like this, you can just stuff it back down your craw. It's either this, or you really hang. As for your indictment, we'll search every cowboy and whore you've ever known until we find it. And it won't take long, either."

Stain turned his gaze onto Coble and said: "The only reason we've gone along with your blackmail is sitting right at this table. John Coble. For some strange reason, you've managed to make a true friend in this life. Coble's defended you in everything you've done. He doesn't want you to die. So we're doing this for him."

Horn erupted in bitter laughter. "Oh, that's quite a fine speech, Stain. You're so full a shit, it's comin' outta your ears. The only reason you'd even consider freein' me is because I've got the goods on you. Don't give me any more of that nobility bullshit."

Coble broke in, saying: "Now, now. This doesn't do nobody no good. Here's the facts. Tom, this harebrained scheme works. I know, 'cause I tried it. Now, you're not gonna know until that trap door falls away whether the powers that be have really let you go. You're either gonna fall into a wagon, or fall into eternity. These days I 'spect one's about as good as the other. I trust these men, Tom. I have to. They've said they'll spring you, and they will. But you've gotta judge for yourself whether to trust 'em or not. You've got an indictment floatin' around somewhere out there that could bring the whole cattle industry down. Even if the court wouldn't take the charges seriously, the newspapers would. The people o' this state would start shootin' at each and every one of us. It seems as if you've got us over a barrel, Tom."

Horn clenched his shackled hands, forcing his fingernails into his palms. He absorbed the silence in the room, broken only by Clay Stephens's heavy breathing. Pushing back on the chair and standing, he said: "All right."

Stain seemed to ease back in his chair and stroked his chin. He coughed lightly and broke the silence. "So, we have but one more bit of business to take care of. You need to let whoever has your so-called indictment know that you've cheated the devil. What if you're off gallivanting around Mexico and the note is still delivered?"

"It won't be," said Horn. "If I contact whoever's holding the note within three months, it'll be destroyed and never sent. If I don't, it'll be on its way. It's that simple."

"When are you planning on making the contact?" Stain countered. "I don't believe any of us are up to sitting on pins and needles through the spring."

"I could care less what you sit on, Stain," Horn spat. "Take it or leave it."

Stain's face grew red, and he started to respond, but, instead, he stood, donned his coat, and stepped out into the cold.

A moment later, Horn gestured at Stephens and said: "Take me back to my cell."

Hugh Carey was scared. He didn't know exactly why, but he knew he was scared. First, the schoolmarm came strolling into the livery stable like she owned the place, newly fallen snow on her velvet coat and hat. She up and hands him a note from Horn that was marked personal, but he felt, from looking at her too-blank expression, that she had read it. Then, no sooner than she left and he read the note, Frank Webster and two drovers came walking in, asking him about the schoolmarm, what she wanted. He had never considered himself a good liar, but found himself telling the cattleman he had contacted her earlier about taking some French lessons. He had always wanted to go to Paris, he said, and planned on it, someday, if he ever saved up enough money. He thought she could help him out. She had come down to talk to him about it, he said.

Webster had looked at him doubtfully, then turned to leave. He turned back around and began to say something, then stopped. He merely turned and left.

Carey knew something was wrong, very wrong. He had put Horn's letter to the prosecutor behind a loose brick in the foundation of the bunkhouse, back on Webster's spread. He didn't know what it said, but he knew that it must be of great importance. Horn's new note only served to confuse him. Now he was supposed to wait three months to contact the prosecutor after Horn was dead. Why? What was going on?

The next day, Carey went to the jail to see Horn. Clay Stephens said the prisoner couldn't take visitors, unless Carey was a bona-fide preacher. Not even the schoolmarm, who he'd turned away that morning. Tom's visiting days were over, he said. Carey walked outside and around the back to the privy. He entered, pulled the note the schoolmarm had delivered from his waistcoat pocket, and threw it down the hole.

The following day, he took off from the ranch by himself, checking out strays in a series of shallow arroyos to the south. He rode for about two hours before cutting up one cañon, following the tracks of three or four steers. He rounded them up and was heading back out when he looked across the prairie and saw three riders approaching in the distance.

"God damn, Tom," he whispered to himself. "I don't know what you got me into."

Chapter Sixteen

The morning of his hanging, Tom Horn awoke to find he had slept the night through for the first time in two months. He'd closed his eyes about midnight and awoke to the dawn without dreams. Willie Nickell had not visited, and his blankets weren't covered with sweat.

He had a lump in his throat the size of a red apple, and his chest burned with foreboding, but he knew he could do nothing but go through with the plan outlined by Stephens. In the deepest recesses of his consciousness, he really didn't believe the whole thing would work, but the gambler in him forced him to be intrigued.

As he lay on his cot, he thought for the thousandth time of all the things that could go wrong. The worst, of course, was if the cattlemen had no intention of not hanging him, that they would merely throw the noose over his head and let him strangle to death, preferring to allow his accusations to reach the federal prosecutor and deal with them at that time. And then there was the foolish contraption Stephens thought up. Flour sacks and slipknots. He closed his eyes and let out a deep breath, just thinking about it.

His deal with the cattlemen was simple, when it came right down to it. Once the hanging was faked, they would provide him with a horse, his rifle, enough supplies to last a week, and $10,000. He, in turn, would ride south, avoiding civilization until he reached Nogales. He would cross over to the Mexican side and buy some property, becoming another wealthy *gringo* who the natives would think was an expatriate.

All so simple, all so smooth, thought Horn. But he knew that something had to go wrong. It always did. He just hoped it didn't have anything to do with the rope.

Lying on the cot, watching the first tentative rays of light escape from the gray dawn and beam into his cell, he still couldn't believe he'd gone through with the plan. When he thought deeply about it, he felt he could have had it changed. If he'd pushed, they probably would have found another way, despite any protestations. But he balanced the enormity of his crime against the difficulty of actually living through the day, and felt it was all he deserved. In the end, he bought off on the plan precisely because it *wasn't* foolproof, because it required risk. He figured that a chance, a simple chance, was all a man could ask for. Especially a man who had killed a boy.

He thought about escaping to Mexico, and whether he would actually contact Hugh Carey from there, telling him to destroy the evidential note. He supposed he would, not from any love for the cattlemen involved, but for his friendship with John Coble. He knew even though Coble was not named or implicated in any way, the law would still touch him. Others would testify to his complicity. Others would lie to save their own skins. Yes, Horn would contact Carey, but only to save Coble.

As the cell grew almost imperceptibly lighter, Horn rose and paced for a few minutes before splashing cold water on his face and running his hands through his hair. He reached under the bunk and pulled out a wooden box that contained his writing materials and wrote a short note to John Coble, thanking the man for everything, whether or not the gambit that was to unfold that day was successful or not. He then put a note on top of the autobiography he'd been writing, asking Clay Stephens to make sure the schoolmarm received the manuscript.

The schoolmarm. His features tightened up as he thought of her, conjured up her smooth skin and deep eyes. He would never see her again, he knew. He also knew he would have to fight the urge to contact her, instead enduring the long Mexican evenings with his memories for comfort. Leaving her the manuscript would cement his "death." He smiled bitterly at the thought that he would perhaps live to see his own autobiography in print, providing that Glendolene Kimmell could sell the musings. He hoped she would, and that she would benefit financially. He had nothing else to leave her.

He continued to pace the cell, working off nervous energy, as the dawn rose on a cold, gray day. The wind intermittently pounded the side of the building. *Tame by Cheyenne standards,* he thought. But it made him think, anyway. He hoped they would pack a good hat with a tight fit. He'd need it in this wind.

As the dawn burst over the horizon, Frank Webster walked out of his ranch house, headed for the saddled horse at ready in the barn. A few hours before, he had found what he had searched for over the previous three days. He had found an envelope shoved behind a loose brick on the outside of his bunkhouse. He had found the way to ensure Horn's silence.

The anxiety of the past few days had taken its toll on the big cattleman. Since he had seen Glendolene Kimmell walk from the livery after talking with Hugh Carey, his life had been miserable. One of his men had been tailing her, keeping to the shadows as she visited Horn at the jail, and then as she walked to the general store. Webster made sure he was on the street when she emerged, intending to engage her in conversation about Horn. Instead, she asked him about Hugh Carey, which surprised him. He told her that Carey was at the livery, and watched her walk the two blocks to the stable. He stood there, not knowing what to do, until Clay Stephens caught up with him, telling him that it seemed as if either the schoolmarm or Carey were likely to be holding Horn's mysterious missive. Of course, each of the affected cattlemen had suspected Miss Kimmell from the beginning, but couldn't find any evidence, even after carefully rifling her belongings at Jim Miller's ranch. Even John Coble's careful questioning only brought blank stares. He, at least, believed she knew nothing about it.

Hugh Carey, on the other hand, was a complete surprise. An excellent cowboy, Carey was quiet and reserved. He was known to be friendly with Horn, although not overly so. But Stephens noted that Carey had dropped by several times over the past couple of months, and seemed particularly skittish after visiting just before Horn announced that he wanted to avoid the hangman, after all.

After the schoolmarm had come back out of the stable, Webster and two of his hands, Jim Parker and Harlan Quayle, had walked into the stable and confronted Carey. The cowboy had looked shaken, and had told them some cock-and-bull story about wanting to learn French from the schoolmarm. The next morning, just to make sure, Webster had stopped by the Miller spread, ostensibly on business. After talking with Jim Miller about the weather and such, Webster had watched as the schoolmarm emerged, ready to be driven to the school. Webster had smiled, tipped his hat, and, in French, said: "Good morning, Miss Kimmell. How are you today?"

The schoolmarm had looked at him with a mischievous grin and said: "Why Mister Webster, how charming! I didn't know you spoke French!"

"Well, yes, ma'am," he had answered. "My mother was French, and I grew up with it. Perhaps we could have a conversation some time, just to keep me brushed up."

"It's a lovely idea, sir, but I must confess that my understanding of French extends to a few words, only." She had cocked her head, smiled, and said: "Now, if German is your cup of tea, we can talk until the cows come home, *Herr* Webster!"

Webster had managed a weak smile and said: "No, I don't suppose so, miss. I'll just have to carry on talkin' to myself, I suppose."

Having established that Carey had lied, Webster had returned to his spread and torn apart Carey's bunk. He had found nothing.

The next day, at wit's end, he had gathered Parker and Quayle and followed Carey out onto the prairie. They had found him at the mouth of an arroyo, herding some strays. Webster had asked him to dismount so they could talk. The cowboy warily did so, joining the three other men near a thicket of scrub oak.

"Hugh, it seems you told me a story a couple of days ago. You see, Miss Kimmell might look like she just danced off the line of some Paris girlie show, but she doesn't speak much French. Certainly not enough to teach you anything."

Carey had swallowed hard and managed to stare at Webster. The big man had met his gaze with fire in his eyes.

"Tom Horn gave you something, Hugh. I want it."

Responding quickly, Carey had said: "I don't have

nothin' of Tom's, Mister Webster. Nothin' at all."

The first punch had hit him so hard he was sure it had broken his jaw, but he had stood up, only to be hit again. Then again and again.

A half hour later, beaten and bloodied by the fists of the two cowhands, Carey had tried to gather his senses and run for his horse to get away. He had not talked, hadn't spoken a word other than a few screamed expletives, in fact, and sworn to himself that he wouldn't, under any circumstances. *By God,* he had said to himself, *a man has few friends in life, and not enough time to betray them.*

Parker had quickly mounted his horse and roped the running Carey. At Webster's nod, he had taken off across the prairie, dragging the cowboy behind. He had purposely led his horse through scrub oak and yucca, and, when he had returned, Carey was nearly unrecognizable. Great strips of skin had been ripped from his face, and several of his fingers were broken, sticking out from his hands at odd angles. Broken yucca spines protruded from his neck and scalp.

Webster had tried again, leaning down to the suffering cowboy and asking about Horn's letter to the prosecutor. Carey had lain there as Webster's fury grew. At length, the vicious kicks from the three men's boots had begun to hurt less, and he knew he was dying. He had been relieved when he heard the pistol cock and looked up at the barrel pointed between his eyes.

"One more chance, Hugh," Webster had hissed.

Carey had merely closed his eyes and waited.

Later, Webster had torn apart the bunkhouse again, figuring that what few valuable possessions Carey had must be there somewhere. His cowboys who weren't on the range had helped, and in no time the place looked like an artillery shell had landed in its midst.

Well after midnight, one of the cowboys on his way to the privy had noticed a brick without mortar in the outside foundation. He carried a lantern closer and saw the brick was loose. He managed to get his fingers around its perimeter and slowly work it out, dropping it to the side. In the space were concealed a locket with a photograph of a young woman, $75 dollars in cash, a $100 confederate note, and an envelope. He had yelled for Webster.

After reading the affidavit and realizing that Horn truly could have caused immense trouble for livestock interests, Webster had mounted his horse and headed for Cheyenne. It seemed as if there would be a hanging, after all.

Two hours later, he had pulled up before John Stain's house and entered. Stain had been surprised to see him, and even more surprised to find that Horn's missive had been located. While reading the note, his face had turned beet red, and his hands had shaken uncontrollably. He set the letter down on a darkly stained table and poured himself and Webster two fingers of brandy each. They had both shot it back quickly.

An hour later, Clay Stephens, Peter Cooper, and Dave James joined Stain and Webster in Stain's office. Grim faced, Webster told the men about finding the envelope, leaving out Hugh Carey's fate.

"It's good that we found it now, Frank," said Dave James. "Good work. Now we can hang Horn and be done with it."

"Right," said Cooper. "I guess Tom's in for a bit of a surprise." Then, wistfully, he said: "I can't say as that I'm happy this is occurin', though. I always had a likin' for Tom."

"I don't think we oughta hang him," said Stephens. The other three men began to protest loudly. The sheriff merely sat mute until they calmed down. Then he said: "Now listen! Tom Horn might be a killer and a blackmailer, but he's nobody's fool. If Peter and I walk him up that gallows and he thinks anything is wrong, he'll be suspicious, all right. I'll guarantee you he'll get loud as all get out. The last thing we need is someone screamin' and hollerin' about how you cattle boys had folks killed all over the country. No, I think we oughta let things go on as planned, and handle Tom Horn in another way."

John Stain nodded and said: "I tend to agree, Clay. But how?"

As Stephens began outlining the amended plan for Tom Horn's demise, Stain refilled his glass with the robust brandy. He would need it this day, he thought.

Horn was surprised when his knees almost buckled as Clay Stephens entered his cell with two deputies. He hadn't counted on showing any weakness, particularly to Stephens, a man who wouldn't have lasted a month in the Arizona campaign, according to Horn's estimation. Yet, his body betrayed him, and he couldn't stop the anxiety. He was nearly certain that Stephens's plan wouldn't work, that something would go wrong. Yet, he'd forced himself to go along with it, to gamble with his life.

"Tom, it's time," said Stephens. "You're sure you don't want no preacher? Somebody to talk about yer soul and such?"

"No, Clay," answered Horn, "I suspect I've talked to the good Lord about as much as common in my life." For the benefit of the deputies, he added: "I don't suppose I'll be seein' him too soon, do you, Clay."

"Depends, Tom, depends," said Stephens. "He may be waitin' with open arms, who knows."

Under his breath, for only Stephens to hear, Horn mumbled: "Well, God'd better be a Messican, then, Clay." Shooting the sheriff a hard stare, he said: "Understand?"

Stephens merely took Horn by the shoulder and gently turned him toward the cell wall. "I'm gonna tie your hands, here, Tom," he said.

Horn nearly jumped when one of the deputies offered Stephens his handcuffs, but Stephens pleasantly replied that he would use a common old rope to tie Horn's hands. It seemed more fitting, he commented.

Walking from the cell for the final time, Horn couldn't help but feel an incredible rush of freedom. In an hour, he'd either be visiting with the devil or on his way to Mexico. Strangely he thought to himself that he couldn't wait to see how it all turned out.

The four men walked down the creaking stairs to Stephens's office, then entered a door in the back of the room that Horn had never been through. A short corridor was ahead, then another open door. Through the door, Horn glimpsed the bright color of freshly cut pine contrasted by black, funereal cloth. As they approached, he thought that the gallows looked absolutely unlike the one he feared so much in his dream. It was not as big, not as imposing. Yet, he couldn't help but cast a quick look about for a boy holding a noose.

The room they entered was huge and held about thirty people; each was dressed somberly. Horn knew most of the men, and saw them look anxiously at him. As he entered, the soft buzz of conversation quit, and all eyes were on him. He nodded to several of the men and saw them nervously nod back.

He was escorted across the front of the gallows, the light color of his prison-issue clothing contrasting with the dense black of the drape. He subdued the urge to push against the drape with his shoulder, to see if a wagon had truly been concealed there.

His wits seemed to have been sharpened, and he mentally checked each detail of the structure for any variance in Stephens's plan. Thus far, it looked as if the sheriff had kept his word. The drape was high, and would certainly hide a swinging body from sight. He began to feel a little more confident.

The deputies stopped at the bottom of the stairway that led to the gallows' platform. Stephens continued to guide Horn up the stairs where, almost a surprise, Peter Cooper waited rather than the boy, Willie Nickell. Horn smiled grimly to himself and fought to keep his self-control.

As they reached the platform, Horn looked behind the draping and noticed with satisfaction the two flour sacks perched on the back of the trap door. They were tied together with a short rope extending from the top. The end of the rope was tied to a sturdy metal clasp of the kind used to secure harness rings together.

The noose itself hung over an eight-by-eight beam directly above the trap door. Horn was uneasy looking at the coiled loop. To him, it seemed to be a regular noose, with no possibility of slipping. But, of course, that was the idea.

Stephens led Horn behind the drape and positioned him on the trap door. Horn felt the wood give slightly beneath him, and an electric current seemed to buzz throughout his body. He found he was breathing quickly and used every ounce of self-control he could muster to settle himself down.

Stephens reached up and lowered the noose over Horn's head, securing the knot on the side. The rope lay directly against the stiff collar he had donned underneath the buttoned shirt. As soon as the noose was in place, Horn felt Stephens pat his hands from behind. He stretched them and found that the rope binding his hands fell away. He believed! There was no way they could hang him without his hands bound. He would grab the noose and hold on. They were going through with the sham!

As he stood, looking out over the drape at the crowd before him, he felt Stephens hook something onto the rope behind his neck, out of sight of the assemblage. Stephens stepped away.

Stephens cleared his throat in the silence and said: "Tom, these men are here to witness your execution for the killing of Willie Nickell. Do you have any last words?"

Horn took a deep breath and felt himself pull slightly against the pressure of the noose. "Only that I've rode the trails with many of you. You're good men and good friends, and I'll see you on down the road."

The men in the crowd looked nervously at Horn, some of them wiping moisture from their eyes. Their solemnity seemed nearly tactile, as if it could nearly be seen in the room as they looked at the man most had known, and some had liked. Now standing before them on the platform with a noose around his neck, he would cease to exist in a moment. It was hard to fathom. Most felt lucky that the drape would stop them from having to see his death throes.

Swallowing hard, Horn turned toward Stephens and said: "Let's get on with it."

Out of the corner of his eye, he watched Stephens and Cooper walk to the edge of the platform, where the lever that activated the trap door was mounted. It took every bit of control not to bring his hands forward and grab the noose, but he managed to hold them behind his back. He nodded at Stephens, and watched the sheriff jerk back on the lever. Then, he was falling into the abyss, his hands lurching up to his neck, only to find the noose slipping off as his weight carried him through the trap door. He landed with a soft *thud* in the dark and rolled into what he felt to be several feet of loose hay. Quietly rubbing the dust and pieces of hay from his eyes, he looked above him, where he saw the two flour sacks twisting slowly, causing the beam above to creak. It was incredibly quiet.

It had worked!

Above, he saw Stephens and Doc Price bend over, ostensibly to check the body. At length, he watched them stand erect again. The doctor said something quietly in Stephens's ear, and Horn heard the sheriff announce: "Gentlemen. Tom Horn is dead. You've witnessed his execution. It's done."

It all happened quickly after that. He waited for Cooper and Stephens to lower the flour sacks and quietly bury them under the hay in the corner of the wagon. He then did the same himself, pulling his shirt up over his face to aid in breathing and resting his head against one of the sacks.

Soon he heard men sliding a coffin into the wagon, and felt an eerie sensation as he reached over and touched the rough planed wood, knowing that someone who resembled him was thawing out inside.

He barely noticed the stop at the train station, where the coffin was unloaded. He found it hard to breathe through the straw, and several times had to stifle sneezes. When the wagon took off again, he realized he was freezing cold. He wore only a thin prison-issue denim shirt and broadcloth trousers. By the time he figured they were on the outskirts of Cheyenne, he thought he might be frozen solid. Yet, the wagon continued on the rough, rutted road toward John Coble's ranch. He couldn't risk talking or otherwise let the driver know he was there for fear that the man hadn't been briefed as to his presence. He hoped that the wagon would stop and Stephens or Coble would let him know things were running smoothly. But no assurance came.

Two excruciatingly uncomfortable hours later, the wagon arrived in the yard of John Coble's ranch.

When the wagon came to a stop, Horn remained still until he heard Coble's voice. "Tom," he said, "if you haven't froze to death, jump on up."

Horn immediately began to flex his cramped muscles as he sat up, clawing his way through the hay and straw above him. He stood and looked about. As he brushed the straw from his head and shoulders, he saw John Coble, standing next to the wagon, smiling up at him. John Stain and Peter Cooper were mounted a few feet away. Old Dave James leaned against the front of the wagon with Frank Webster. He couldn't help smiling at Coble and spreading his grin over the entire group.

He continued to brush straw from himself and stepped over the sideboard of the wagon and jumped to the ground. "Clay," he said, "I've got to admit, I was a mite jumpy over this whole thing. But it worked like a charm, didn't it?"

Clay Stephens favored Horn with a steely stare and said: "Yeah, it sure did, Tom. I told you so." He took a deep breath and added: "Yep, it worked just fine."

Coble had walked to the front of the wagon, joining James and Webster. His smile was nearly as wide as Horn's as he said: "Tom, it looks like you beat the devil after all. Lemme go get your horse. I imagine Mexico's waitin'."

Coble walked toward a nearby corral where a saddled horse stood, tethered to a post. At the same time, Stain dismounted and tied his horse to the wagon's gate. He removed a saddlebag and slung it over his shoulder. Horn watched him warily.

"Tom, is there anything else you need?" asked Stain.

"Just a coat, Stain. I'm freezin' to death."

"Well, that won't be a problem where you're going now, will it?"

"Nope," answered Horn, on edge. "Mexico's warm pretty near 'bout all the time."

Stain smiled grimly as he said through clenched teeth: "It's not Mexico I'm thinkin' of, Tom."

Stain reached into the saddlebag and brought out a piece of leather, a belt Horn figured. Looking closer, he nearly gasped. The hair stood up on the back of his neck as he realized John Stain held Hugh Carey's belt, dangling it before him like the Apaches used to dangle enemy scalps.

"Yes, we found your information, Tom," he said. "Frank here couldn't convince Hugh Carey to squawk, but he managed to find it, anyway."

Horn looked at Webster with hate in his eyes. "So you killed Hugh, Frank?" he said malevolently. "There was no need for that. No need at all!"

Webster merely stared back, then turned his head toward the corral where Coble was returning with the horse.

Sensing something wrong, Coble dropped the horse's reins and shouted: "What's happening here? What's going on?"

Stain answered Coble, all the while looking at Horn. "John," he said, "we couldn't really let Tom go. You must know that. He'd go through ten grand and be back here to blackmail us in no time. We found the indictment he prepared, John. Now, we have to take care of him."

"Who does?" Coble asked, incredulity in his voice.

"Me," said Stain. "If I must, I will."

"No!" screamed John Coble. "I won't have this. . . ."

Horn instinctively jumped at Stain just as the man pulled a well-worn Colt from the saddlebag. He saw he had no chance, but rushed Stain anyway, hoping at least to deflect the path of a shot. Stain immediately backed up two steps and fired, catching Horn on the side of the neck and spinning him to his right. Horn fought to regain his balance and jump toward Stain, suddenly feeling as if the whole world had slowed down, as if everyone was moving at half speed. He could feel every fiber of his being straining to close the gap between himself and Stain, but, as if in a dream, his muscles would not respond. Stain was tantalizingly close, yet as far away as Denver. He watched as Stain, his eyes fearful and his lips pulled back in a feral grin, slowly pulled the trigger again. Horn wondered if he would see the bullet emerge from the barrel just as the second shot crashed through his chest.

Then there was silence. Silence except for the breeze gently blowing through the posts of the corral.

There was no pain, as he thought there would be. He'd been shot before, and there had always been pain. In fact, he wondered if Stain had missed. When he tried to rise, he found that he could not move. Above him, he saw John Coble kneel down and gingerly lift his head and lay it on something soft. *Probably his coat,* Horn thought. *John's the kind who would put his coat under your head. He'd let you rest when you're tired.*

Looking up, he couldn't quite understand what his friend was saying, but he knew they were words of encouragement. He wanted to tell John that everything was all right. He wanted to tell him the boy was waiting next to the wagon, waiting patiently. Willie smiled this time without animosity, and didn't hold a rope. He was just waiting.

Waiting for Horn to follow him.

"As soon as I can move, I'll be along," Horn whispered, his soft words being swept away by the wind. "I got to tell you somethin', Willie boy. It was a mistake. I didn't mean it, boy."

Willie just grinned.

John Stain rode alone across the prairie north of Cheyenne. He needed time to think, to allow the great wide country to numb his soul and perhaps soothe his emotions. He had rarely killed before and found it absolutely disturbing. He would not do it again, he told himself. Under any circumstances.

When the buildings of Cheyenne were visible in the distance, he pulled up his horse near one of the few trees that grew on the harsh prairie. He produced a long cigar from his waistcoat pocket, along with a match, flicking it against his fingernail. Cupping his hands, he lit the cigar and puffed softly for a few moments. Dismounting, he walked to the cottonwood's lee side, attempting to shield himself from the cold, gusty wind that had picked up over the last couple of hours.

He hunkered in at the base of the tree, pulling his coat wide to diminish the effects of the wind and create a calm spot before him. He puffed furiously on the cigar as he reached in the inside pocket of his canvas overcoat and withdrew Tom Horn's indictment of Wyoming's cattle interests. After reading the missive one last time, he took the first brittle page and crumpled it somewhat. He then pulled the cigar from his mouth and touched its red-hot ash to the paper. As soon as it was on fire, he continued with the second page, then the third, then the fourth. When they were destroyed, he stood, and walked back to his horse. Before mounting, he looked back toward the cottonwood and watched the ashes begin to blow across the brown prairie. As he mounted his horse and loped off toward Cheyenne, the ashes were picked up and carried high over the ground below, scattered to the earth's four corners by the Wyoming wind.

Epilogue

Elko, Nevada 1914

John Coble sat firmly ensconced in an overstuffed chair in the hotel lobby. His joints were racked with pain from decades of riding horseback, and he felt as if he were the oldest man in the world. Lately it seemed harder to travel away from Iron Mountain on business, and more meaningless, too.

About a year before, something odd had happened. He had returned from John Stain's funeral and thrown his good jacket across his bed. He sat in a wooden rocking chair in the room and glanced out the window. There, riding across the prairie was a cowboy herding a group of steers. Thinking about the funeral and counting the black marks on John Stain's soul, he didn't notice the rider at first, but something about the way he held himself brought it all back. He stood and stared for a moment, then rushed to the door and out into the yard. He sprinted as far as his aging legs could carry him around the old bunkhouse. The cowboy sat on his horse, startled by the panting old man before him.

"Mister Coble?" the 'puncher queried. "Somethin' wrong, Mister Coble?"

Seeing the cowhand was a young man he'd hired a few weeks earlier, he merely shook his head and said: "No, son.

No. I just, um, thought you were someone else for a minute."

Over the months, he thought he saw the familiar rider several times, covering the wide prairie on a fast horse. He didn't know what to think of the apparition, but he thought he understood it. He realized long ago that he would never rid himself of the immense guilt he felt over Horn's death. He hadn't even tried. For eleven years it had eaten at him, and there were times when it was difficult, indeed, to keep the oath of silence he'd bitterly sworn with Stain and the others.

Occasionally, he would ride by the unmarked grave on the prairie and doff his hat for a moment out of respect for his friend. Some of his cowhands had noticed and asked if there was something special about the spot. He'd said no, that he was just admiring the countryside.

He'd had time to think in Elko. The previous month of buying cattle and returning to his room alone had taken its toll. He found himself reminiscing and thinking about what might have been. His body ached, and he admitted that his soul ached as well. It begged for release. It begged for forgiveness.

A single tear ran down the old man's cheek as he sat in the comfortable chair. He watched the dust motes slowly descend through a spear of light shooting across the center of the room, and he remembered his friend for the last time before sliding the barrel of the old Colt into his mouth and gently squeezing the trigger.

Author's Note

Wyoming Wind is a work of fiction. Although many of the characters are historical in nature and made their marks on the western United States and Wyoming in particular, their adventures chronicled here are, for the most part, the author's inventions. Most of the characters are likewise the author's creations.

For definitive studies of the real Tom Horn and his times, I encourage you to pick up Chip Carlson's detailed *Tom Horn: Killing Men Is My Specialty* published by Beartooth Corral, Cheyenne, Wyoming. Dean Krakel's *The Saga of Tom Horn: The Story of a Cattleman's War* is also highly recommended.

Although Horn was posthumously acquitted of Willie Nickell's murder in September, 1993, the famous confession coerced by Joe LeFors still remains a powerful indictment. Obtained illegally, and perhaps while Horn was under the influence of excessive amounts of rotgut, the language, nonetheless, has a flow that suggests the confession was not, as Horn maintained later, the invention of hidden stenographer Charlie Ohnhaus.

When judging the historical Tom Horn, one has but to read the disputed confession to find the origins of the black image that followed Horn to the grave and beyond.

JOE LEFORS: "How far was Willie Nickell killed?"

TOM HORN: "About three hundred yards. It was the best shot that I ever made and the dirtiest trick I ever done."

The demise of Tom Horn on the plains outside of Cheyenne at the hands of cattlemen is not my invention. Although most with an interest in the Horn case believe he met his doom on the gallows, some alleged descendants of Wyoming's turn-of-the-century cattlemen accept the possibility that Horn was reprieved, only to be betrayed and killed. Although historical evidence would seem to refute such an occurrence, I think it's a dandy rumor.

DOUBLE EAGLES
ANDREW J. FENADY

Captain Thomas Gunnison has been entrusted with an extremely vital cargo. His commerce ship, the *Phantom Hope*, is laden with two thousand Henry rifles, weapons that could turn the tide of victory for the Union. Even more important, though, is fifteen million dollars in newly minted double eagles, money the Union needs to finance the war effort. So when the *Phantom Hope* is attacked and crippled, Gunnison makes the only possible decision—he and his men will transport the gold across the rugged landscape of Mexico, to Vera Cruz. Gunnison's caravan could change the course of history . . . if bloodthirsty Mexican guerrillas and Rebel soldiers don't stop it first!

JANE CANDIA COLEMAN

BORDERLANDS

In this thrilling collection of brilliant short stories, award-winning author Jane Candia Coleman takes us on an exciting tour of the different borderlands of the Old West, some real, some emotional, borderlands that mark endings . . . but also beginnings. From settlers on the Montana-Canada border to Pancho Villa's bold attack on New Mexico, these tales tell of daring and courage, adventure and danger. They feature journeys made by people looking for a better life, to escape an old life—or simply to stay alive.

G. G. BOYER

WINCHESTER AFFIDAVIT

The New Mexico Territory is bleeding in the throes of the Amarillo War, named for the vast estate known as the Amarillo Grant. The estate manager's *segundo* leads a group of night riders known as the Whitecaps, who use violence and mayhem to brutally clear the grant of "squatters," homesteaders and ranchers just trying to make lives for themselves. Cleve Bandelier, former cavalry officer and widowed father of two, leads the group of ranchers that the Whitecaps are forcing off the land. But Cleve will need all the strength and courage he can muster if he hopes to stand up for long against the corruption, brute force . . . and murder.